THE PROTECTOR'S EMERALD

BOOK 4 of OCTOBERS

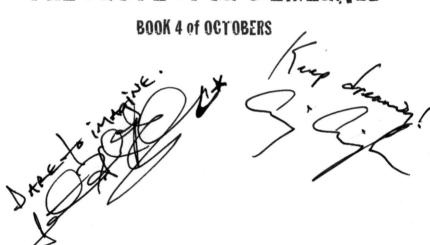

www.theoctobers.com

MOONSUNG

presents

THE PROTECTOR'S EMERALD

BOOK 4 of OCTOBERS

FROM THE IMAGINATIONS OF
J.H. REYNOLDS AND CRAIG CUNNINGHAM

ILLUSTRATIONS BY J.R. FLEMING

Text copyright © 2011 J.H. Reynolds
Illustrations and cover painting by J.R. Fleming
All rights reserved. Published by Moonsung, Inc.
MOONSUNG and associated logos
are trademarks of Moonsung, Inc.

www.moonsungbooks.com

OCTOBERS, characters, names, and related indicia
are trademarks and © of J.H. Reynolds

No part of this publication may be re-produced, stored in
a retrieval system, or transmitted in any form or by any
means, electronic, mechanical, photocopying, recording,
or otherwise, without written permission of the publisher.
For information regarding permission, contact MOONSUNG:
general@moonsungbooks.com

ISBN 978-0615544809

Dedicated to our readers,
for daring to imagine.

CONTENTS

In the town of Hobble, October never ends . . .

THE PROTECTOR'S EMERALD

BOOK 4 of OCTOBERS

31 Days Before . . .

Chapter 1:

Only The Beasts Knew The Secret

Happy Gumbledump and Guffy Tinklepot stood guard at the Crescent Gates, loyal to the duty to which they had been devoted for fifty years, and awaited the arrival of the New Year.

Scents of apple cider and pecan pies drifted by as the two old men admired the jack o' lantern moon descending toward the western horizon. Nearby, costumed Hobblers skipped across the shingled rooftops of Town Square, carrying lanterns and candy-buckets. The New Year was only moments away, and everyone in town gathered their things and followed the trail of Jypsi carriages toward the festival field, where the annual tournaments and competitions would be held.

The two gatekeepers rolled a pair of dice out of Guffy's black tricorn hat, and cheered when double sixes appeared, staring back at them like twin destinies. Not a moment later, the Clock Tower struck midnight, and the merry old men hurrahed at the hypnotic fireworks which exploded above the distant festival field, signaling that the annual Star Festival had begun.

"Time to conduct the Lighting!" Guffy proclaimed.

He slid the dice into his coat pocket and placed his tricorn hat back atop his cottony head as he walked toward the stone wall.

Happy lit a torch and carried it over to the wall. One of Happy's eyes was as wide as a moon, but the other was covered by a black patch, the result of a childhood accident that had left him half blind.

The cheerful gatekeeper reminisced to Guffy, "I reckon we've spent more of our lives at this gate than anywhere else. We was just boys when we began our apprenticeship."

Happy climbed onto Guffy's frail shoulders and faced the year's final lantern, which glowed atop the crescent-shaped gate like a captured star. The one-eyed man took a deep breath, and extinguished the lantern. The past twelve Octobers were over, and a new twelve had arrived.

Happy re-lit all twelve lanterns, as he and Guffy sang the traditional Lighting Carol for the fiftieth year in a row . . .

All Hallows Eve whispers goodbye,
The next twelve Octobers' arrival is nigh,
One by one, the Light is reborn,
The lanterns are lit, and the Darkness is torn.

After lighting the final lantern, the soft glow

illuminated the gatekeepers' withered faces as they stared in awe at the meteorite shower which had appeared in the sky above Hobble at the stroke of midnight.

But Guffy's smile soon dimmed as he recalled the strange tidings he had received earlier that evening—tidings he did not want to believe were true.

He addressed his comrade in a solemn tone, "Have you heard the news, Gumbledump?"

Happy wiped his hands on his trousers.

"What news?"

"The council's secret," Guffy whispered.

"Hadn't heard no secrets," Happy replied, concealing the secret which he had kept hidden for fifty years—a secret for which he would give his life.

"The Black Candle's been stolen. Someone betrayed the secret of the crypt," Guffy revealed.

Happy's eye goggled. He lifted up his shirt and revealed the black mark—a circle surrounded by twelve dots— branded into his flesh long ago. "But the ark in the crypt was sealed! We were both there! We saw it shut! We swore the Oath!"

Guffy immediately placed his hand over Happy's mouth.

"Shush! The Lostwood is always listening," Guffy warned. "There's a new strangeness about, just as it was at the beginning of the Old War. Better keep an extra eye out tonight, my old friend."

At Guffy's command, Happy reached into his overcoat pocket, pulled out his glass eye, removed his patch, then popped the shiny globe into his empty socket.

"How's that?" Happy asked with a wink.

—

3

"Pipe down, Happy," Guffy commanded. "I swear, you'd lose your noggin if it weren't attached to your neck."

Right then, an eerie silence spread over the forest like a plague. Happy and Guffy both sensed something unusual in the air.

A scent.

A feeling.

A shiver.

In their many years of standing guard, the greatest dangers they had ever encountered were wild goblins and hoodwinks, and that was only once every dozen moons or so. But on this night, both gatekeepers sensed that whatever approached the Crescent Gates was something much more dangerous.

Suddenly, a thunderous swoosh emanated out of the dark forest, like a blade ripping through the chilly air.

"What was that, Gumbledump?" Guffy asked.

He turned to look at his companion, and convulsed in horror when Happy's head tumbled off his stubby neck and rolled across the ground, stopping against Guffy's black, buckled boots.

Blood poured out of Happy's severed head and formed a crimson pool at Guffy's feet. Ribbons of steam fluttered into the cool night air and dissolved before Guffy's disbelieving eyes.

Guffy squawked in horror, and quickly turned to run for the safety of Town Square. But before he could escape, the swoosh roared out of the Lostwood again and poured its wrath upon the lone gatekeeper.

Guffy's head tumbled off his neck and rolled to a stop in front of Happy's lifeless gaze. For a moment, both headless bodies remained standing at the entrance to Hobble, stunned by their own tragic fates. Then a haunted wind emerged from the Lostwood and blew the corpses to the ground like fallen timbers.

For the first time in fifty years, the Crescent Gates were left unguarded.

Only the beasts knew the secret. They alone had seen *who* had murdered Happy Gumbledump and Guffy Tinklepot.

But no one—not even the beasts—knew Happy's secret. He had done what he had long ago sworn to do—even before he had promised to protect the location of the crypt.

Happy had taken his own secret to his grave.

Chapter 2:

Baskets And Broomsticks

Moony Jarman swept the grubby floors of the Candletin Inn, and dreamed of a day when he would no longer have to toil his hours away while the rest of Hobble basked in festival cheer.

A carnival of jack o' lanterns flickered from the cobwebbed windowsills of the Fireside Room as the stable boy moved through the crowd of New Year's revelers. He wore thick boots and tattered trousers, and the neck of his white cotton shirt was held together by a crisscrossing weave of goblin-hair twine. He gazed out the dusty window at the fireworks exploding above the nearby festival field.

"I know you want to be at the Star Festival, Moony, but it's our busiest night of the year," a soothing voice whispered over Moony's shoulder. "Jypsis and Outskirters pay high token for a soft bed to lay their noggin and a hot meal to warm their bellies. As you know, we need as many tokens as we can muster."

Moony's grandmother, Gem Jarman, walked to the corner of the room and sat down at the family's heirloom piano.

The old woman wore rabbit-foot earrings and a homespun dress the color of a midnight forest. Her braided, silver hair dripped down her back like a ray of moonlight.

The inn's guests—a costumed herd of Hobblers, Jypsis, and Outskirters—danced and drank apple cider while Gem played traditional Hallows Eve songs on the ramshackle instrument, just as she did upon the arrival of every New Year.

Nearby, an Outskirter's elbow knocked a mug off the edge of a table. Without hesitation, Moony turned, reached out his hand, and caught the mug before it shattered upon the ground.

"That's the third mug I've seen you catch tonight, boy," the Outskirter said through his cider-drenched beard. "I dropped that one on purpose, just to see if you'd catch it. You have the keen instincts of a wolf."

Every night, Moony caught countless falling mugs and dishes, and sensed the arrival of guests long before they knocked upon the inn's door.

Moony shrugged his shoulders and placed the mug back on the table. Not a drop of cider had been spilled. He had possessed abnormally quick reflexes for as far back as he could remember, though he had only been able to exercise them during his menial chores at the inn. What he really wanted was to test his abilities at the festival tournaments, especially at the kyteboarding race. He daydreamed about what it might be like to defeat the long-time winner, Red Crisp. But every time a tournament was held, he was needed at the inn.

Still, Moony dreamed of a greater destiny, where his talents, if that's what they were, might truly count for something.

Suddenly, he heard a cough hack through the room of revelry. He picked up his broomstick and walked over to where his little sister, Jezzy, sat alone on the countertop. Her legs dangled off the edge as she muffled her cough with her tiny, pale hands. She wore a silky, pink nightgown, which matched the bright bow in her long, brown hair. While Jezzy coughed and wheezed for breath, she smiled at Moony, revealing where her two front teeth had once been.

"There now, Jezzy," Moony comforted. He felt her sweaty forehead with the palm of his hand, gauging her fever.

Moony looked over at his mother, Beatrice, who squatted next to the fireplace. The beautiful, olive-skinned woman stoked the logs with an iron rod, sending hundreds of tiny sparks floating out of the hearth's mouth and over the guests' heads.

"Mom, Jezzy's been sick for a week, pale as a ghost. We have to get her medicine before she gets worse," Moony urged.

"I've already told you, Moony, we don't yet have enough tokens," Beatrice sighed. "We still owe Mr. Pottleman for last month's rent. And you know how he is about money. Keep socks on her feet and her fingers warm, and let the fever run its course. Simple folks like us have to make do."

Moony nodded in defeat, having heard similar pronouncements his entire life. He lifted Jezzy off the counter and set her down next to the fire cave, where she could stay warm.

"If I had my own tokens, I'd use them to buy you a whole tub of potions," he whispered in her ear.

Moony touched the tip of Jezzy's nose with his fingertip.

"Moony, look!" Jezzy pointed to the far corner of the room.

The stable boy turned just in time to see his grandmother lift a large chocolate cake out of the top of the piano. Twelve sparkling candles glowed atop the silky icing. Gem sang the opening notes of the Hobble Birthday Song, and waved for Moony to join her and the other revelers. He bashfully crossed the room as everyone serenaded him upon the arrival of his twelfth birthday.

After the song ended, Gem nudged Moony with her elbow and encouraged, "Better make it a good wish, boy. You only get one birthday every twelve Octobers."

Moony closed his eyes and repeated the same wish he had made upon every shooting star and upon every coin he had ever tossed into the water well in Town Square.

I wish I could fly.

He blew out all twelve candles, and the room erupted with joyous cheers as both Hobblers and Outskirters lifted their mugs in his honor.

After Moony's birthday celebration was over, he picked up his broomstick and walked out into the cool, candy-scented night.

Laughter sounded from inside the inn, and hurrahs rang out from the distant Star Festival. Half a dozen jack o' lanterns twinkled silently on the wooden steps, where Moony stood all alone. The waterwheel on the side of the inn dipped into Midnight Creek in a steady rhythm, and ribbons of smoke swirled out of the chimney top toward the glittering heavens.

Suddenly, a horse whinnied through the crisp night air. Moony was certain he had stabled all the visitors' horses, but when he looked up, he saw a black mare prancing wildly next to the porch of the inn. The beast bucked its head up and down and side to side.

Two wicker baskets hung over each side of the horse's back, connected by a tattered rope.

Moony approached the horse and softly placed his hand on its neck, calming her into silence. He had always possessed a strange power over animals. For some reason, the beasts trusted him.

"Easy now, girl. I ain't gonna hurt you," he whispered into the horse's perked ear.

Moony cautiously stepped to the side of the frightened beast and lifted the baskets from her back. As soon as he removed the baskets, the mare galloped away like a phantom into the haunted night. Moony could hear the horse's hooves, fading farther and farther into the distance, pattering toward the Crescent Gates.

The two baskets were heavier than Moony expected. As he set them down, he felt something moist seeping out of them. He wiped his hands on his shirt, puzzled at the sticky substance stained onto the fabric.

Moony lifted the lids of both baskets at the same time.

A putrid odor arose from within.

The stable boy covered his nose with his sleeve and cried out at the horrifying sight revealed.

As he staggered back onto the cobbled ground, his feet kicked over the baskets, spilling their contents.

At Moony's feet, staring back at him with cold, glassy eyes, were the bloody, severed heads of Happy Gumbledump and Guffy Tinklepot.

Chapter 3:

The Mysterious Arrival

Guffy Tinklepot's beard was drenched in crimson, and Happy Gumbledump's glass eye stared up at Moony like a frozen moon. Even stranger, there was a bloody **V** carved into both their foreheads. The boy grew cold, and felt his heart pounding inside his chest.

Moony feared nothing more than Death, and avoided even the thought of it at all costs. He refused to set foot in the Hobble Graveyard, and even took the long way home from Town Square in order to avoid passing by Coffdark's Coffin Shop.

And now, Death—his greatest fear—stared back at him with its cruel, unrelenting gaze.

Just then, the doors of the inn swung open, and Tobo Jingles emerged from the pandemonium of laughter coming from within the Fireside Room. He shoved a deck of black cards into his coat pocket, frustrated that his tricks had failed to impress the Jypsis.

The Toymaster nodded at Moony, then squawked like a frightened crow at the sight of the two bloody heads resting against the porch steps.

"It's—it's—" Tobo's voice trembled in horror. "The mark of the Vothlor!"

"Keep quiet, Tobo! You'll scare everyone!" Moony warned, slowly recovering his courage.

The Toymaster flattened himself against the weathered wall of the inn, as if blown by an unseen wind. He covered his pale, quivering mouth with his bony hand.

"But they're—they're—they're *dead*!" the Toymaster stuttered as he pointed in disbelief at the severed heads.

"Something terrible has happened, Tobo," Moony replied. "Go find Mayor Waddletub at the Star Festival. Tell him to meet me on the steps of Town Hall at once."

Tobo closed his eyes and turned his face away, unable to endure the sight.

The stable boy placed his bloodstained hand on Tobo's shoulder, offering him courage. The Toymaster looked into Moony's eyes, then gathered up his valor and ran toward the Star Festival.

"And keep it quiet, Tobo! We don't want to stir the whole town into a panic!" Moony called after him.

Moony watched Tobo run off toward the Star Festival, then slowly turned his eyes back to the horrendous sight which lay before him.

Death, he thought. *This is Death.*

He lifted the two empty baskets, looked around to make sure no one was watching, then nudged the heads back into the baskets with his foot. After closing both lids, he ran toward Town Hall to wait for Mayor Waddletub.

Moony found Town Square empty, save for the Fiddler, who played his haunted tune next to the ancient water well. Moony paced on the front steps of Town Hall beside one of the Immortal Flames. Just then, he heard gentle footsteps behind him and turned to see Principal Lilla Humplestock walk out of Town Hall.

"What're you doing here, boy?" she asked, wiping her hand on her dress. "Why aren't you at the Star Festival with everyone else?"

Moony held the baskets tight to his chest.

"I—I—" he stalled for an explanation. "I'm waiting for someone."

Deep curiosity burned in Principal Humplestock's eyes. She stepped forward, and recoiled in fright at the sight of the blood stained onto Moony's shirt.

"Are you hurt, boy? Where are you bleeding?" She examined him in a panic. "I'll fetch the doctor. Wait here. Everything will be all right."

"I'm fine!" Moony assured, trying to calm her. "It's not *my* blood."

Principal Humplestock's eyes narrowed in confusion.

"Whose is it then?"

Moony looked around to make sure no one was watching.

He slowly lifted the lids of the two wicker baskets. Principal Humplestock turned away and covered her mouth at the gory sight of the rotting faces within.

"Wh—where—where did you find those?" she asked.

Moony covered the baskets, and explained in a cautious

whisper, "Outside the Candletin. I was sweeping the porch, and a rider-less horse galloped up, and—"

Principal Humplestock interrupted before he could finish, "Take them to Coffdark's immediately. The undertaker will keep the—the heads—safe until we can recover the bodies. Go quickly! I must alert Mayor Waddletub right away."

"I've already sent Tobo Jingles to fetch the mayor," Moony told her.

"Hurry, boy! There's no time to waste!" Principal Humplestock urged. Then she whispered in astonished terror, "The Vothlor have returned. It's impossible."

Moony darted from the marble steps of Town Hall toward Coffdark's Coffins. When he was halfway across Town Square, he stopped and looked up at the sky.

A strange, distant roar rattled through the night like an approaching train, growing louder and louder.

Nearer.

And nearer.

Until . . .

A wild light was traveling toward him, growing brighter and louder each moment. Moony sensed it was coming directly toward him.

Just as the light grew as bright as the morning sun, the stable boy leapt behind Town Hall.

The giant fireball landed inside the southern wall of town and charged through the cobbled square like a crazed groundhog, exactly where Moony had been standing. The blaze of light continued to rip a path through the street until it came to a sudden stop in front of the Ministry.

Moony stepped out from the shadows of Town Hall,

and cautiously approached the glowing crater. But when he looked down into the deep cavity, his eyes squinted in disbelief. The meteorite had burned away to nothing, and the crater was entirely empty.

Except for a tiny blue stone.

Chapter 4:

A Broken Covenant

Far away from Town Square, deep in the Lostwood, a hooded figure panted through the dark, purring woods.

It was past the witching hour, long after the annual Star Festival had come to an unexpected conclusion. The yellow eyes of a thousand hidden beasts watched the cloaked stranger as he clawed his way through thickets, brushed past mossy branches, and leapt over fallen logs. The traveler carried with him a secret—one which had haunted him for the fifty years since he had last visited the secret mountain beyond the Bridge of the Covenant.

When he arrived at the Midnight River, the traveler stopped and gazed upon the old bridge in reverent fear, remembering the sacred vows which had long ago been exchanged between the people who lived on each side of the enchanted waters. He knew that crossing to the other side would break the honored covenant.

The rickety bridge creaked beneath his heavy boots as the bubbling voice of the river sang below. The annual meteor shower had been reduced to a few colorful streams of light, illuminating his path toward the yonder mountain.

The hooded man trailed along the mountain's base and gazed up at the dark forest which blanketed its entire face, reaching up toward the vast canvas of glimmering stars.

He cautiously climbed up the side, finally arriving at a small, secret door, nooked into the side of the mountain.

At his knock, a tiny window slid open at the top of the door, and two striking blue eyes appeared.

"Who calls at this late hour?" the woman questioned suspiciously.

The man remained silent as he gazed upon the young woman.

"Speak, or you shall wish you never knocked upon this door," she demanded with fierce eyes.

"I'm—I'm an old friend of your mother's," the man revealed.

The woman squinted in puzzlement.

"My mother has been dead for many years," she replied. "Tell me, how did you find this door?"

The man wanted to say many things to the young woman, but he knew it was not the right time to reveal such secrets.

"I have crossed the Bridge of the Covenant. I come from Hobble."

The woman's eyes widened in terror.

"You lie," she whispered in disbelief. "No one is foolish

enough to cross the Bridge of the Covenant. It's been untouched for fifty years, since the hour of the truce."

"Ay, but it is true. And I did it for reasons which are of interest to you." The man paused, then continued, "For it is beginning again. The mark of the **❢** appeared in Hobble tonight."

The woman blinked in shock.

"The Old War has been awakened," the man continued. "The Black Candle has been stolen and will soon be lit again. Malivar will return—somehow, someway. The time has come for you and your sisters to carry out your mother's will. We must be a part of what is coming."

"How do you know such things?" the woman questioned.

"I know many things," the man answered. "And I know your mother would have warned you of my coming before she died."

The woman peered over her shoulder, as if looking at someone else in the room, then turned back to face the stranger at the door.

"Our mother told us long ago that a strange man might come to this door, seeking our . . . abilities."

"I am that man, and you must obey your mother's instructions."

"What will you have us do then?" the woman asked.

"Bring your magic to Hobble. We must vanish the children of Hobble's future—every last one of them just as it was in the Old War. I have already made the necessary arrangements," the hooded man said, and handed a small scroll through the window.

On the other side of the door, the woman took the papyrus and unrolled it. She examined the list of names, and grew silent for a moment, understanding the task at hand.

"Remove your hood, so that I may see your face," she requested. "Allow me to look into the eyes of one who knew my mother long ago."

The man slowly removed his purple hood, revealing his round, rosy face in the starlight. His head was bald, his waist was rotund, and his eyes were the same as they had been fifty years before when he had last stood before that secret door in the mountain.

A slight smile flickered upon the man's lips as he stepped forward into the lamplight emanating through the small window of the door, and whispered, "Vivy Gubble, you must gather your sisters."

The stranger paused, and stared into the young woman's eyes.

"My name is Winky Waddletub. And I am your father."

Chapter 5:

The Glass Moon

By the next afternoon, Hobble had changed.

News of the gatekeepers' murders and the fallen meteorite had spread throughout the town like a plague. Hobblers walked swiftly down the confetti-covered lanes of Town Square, looking over their shoulders every few steps. Unfounded rumors passed from ear to ear, mostly pure gossip and fiction. But many were certain of one truth: the Vothlor had returned to Hobble.

Some Hobblers accused the Outskirters and Jypsis of committing the murders, reviving old hatreds between the clans. When Sheriff Hopscotch demanded each visitor from outside the walls of Hobble be investigated, nearly every Jypsi and Outskirter left town before noon, offering little cooperation in the hunt for the murderer.

With the sudden exodus of the forest people, the Candletin Inn was full of vacancies once again. After cleaning the stables and brushing the horses, Moony walked into the inn and swept up the remnants of the yesternight's revelry.

Gem sat on a stool next to the hearth, quietly concentrating on her glass blowing. She inserted a long, iron pipe into the fire and then gathered molten glass onto the pipe's end like honey onto a dipper. Then, she gently blew into the mouthpiece of the pipe, causing the molten glass to expand to a silvery bubble. The old woman took a pair of tweezers from her shirt pocket and began forming the glowing fireball into a particular shape.

"How you feeling this afternoon, boy?" Gem called over to Moony.

"I'm fine," Moony lied, still haunted by the night before.

"I'm sorry you had to see such darkness," his grandmother comforted. "You best not dwell on it."

But as Moony looked out the front window to the porch, images of a black horse and soggy wicker baskets crept back into his mind.

"Kel Clovestar stopped by the Inn earlier this morning and told me the strangest thing," Gem said. "Brace yourself, Moony. It's another hubber. Kel said Mayor Waddletub's gone missing."

"What?" Moony turned from the window to face his grandmother.

The old woman continued, "Disappeared soon after the Star Festival came to an abrupt end. Some say he lost courage and went into hiding. Doesn't sound like Winky though. He'd never run from a hubber. Whatever the case, Principal Humplestock is taking his place until he returns."

Moony was stunned.

"Everything's changing so fast, Grammy. Have you ever seen anything like this?"

Gem looked up from her work, and her eyes turned solemn.

She shook her head and replied, "Not since the Old War."

Moony immediately took up his broom, regretting the question. His grandfather, Rufus Jarman, had been killed as a young man at the end of the Old War, and he knew that his grandmother still deeply missed him.

"I don't understand why anyone would do such things," Moony pondered aloud.

"There's much yet to understand, boy, but you're a strong lad—stronger than most grown men. You'll be able to protect yourself, if it comes to it. Believe me, I've been in Hobble for quite some time, and I've never known a boy as remarkable as you."

Gem winked, but Moony did not smile.

"There's nothing *remarkable* about sweeping floors and stabling horses," he replied.

Gem chuckled.

"You sound like your father and grandfather when they were your age. Always dreaming of something more than what was right there in front of them. Your day will come soon enough, Moony. Just wait and see," Gem promised. "For now, do the work that needs to be done."

The old woman nodded toward the broomstick, then stood from her stool and set the glass crescent moon on top of the fireplace mantel. She gazed upon her newest creation for a long moment, and spoke in a soft voice, "By the way,

Mayor Humplestock announced she'll pay one-hundred tokens to whoever can move the fallen meteorite. You should give it a crack, Moony. It never hurts to try."

Gem walked up the creaky stairwell to check on Jezzy, who was in bed in the upstairs apartment. Moony heard his little sister coughing violently.

If I had one-hundred tokens, I could remedy all of my family's problems, he thought.

Moony peered out the dusty window and watched a dozen grown Hobblers try to lift the tiny meteorite from the crater in Town Square. Each Hobbler strained themselves with reddened faces and beastly growls, but the peculiar stone would not budge an inch.

Gem's words echoed in the back of his mind:

For now, do the work that needs to be done.

Without another glance, Moony turned from the window and swept his broom across the floor.

Chapter 6

Skylight Wondering

Moony lay in the barn loft, looking up at the twinkling stars through the open skylight.

The Hobble Star shone directly above the center of town, staring down like a campfire in a faraway world. Moony perused the more distant stars, wondering from which constellation the mysterious meteorite had fallen.

Wind chimes dangled from the straw roof of the cozy barn, and clanked together in the soft breeze. The quiet sounds of the stable wrapped around him like a silken fleece, just as they did every night as he drifted to sleep in his bed of hay. The creaking of the ceiling rafters, the wandering feet of sleepwalking chickens, and the dreamful sighs of slumbering horses had always wooed him into enchanted dreams.

But tonight he could not escape his thoughts about the

meteorite that lay pulsing in Town Square.

It was as if . . . as if it called to him.

Moony sat up, gripped his lantern, and climbed down the rungs of the wooden ladder to the stables below. He tiptoed out the barn doors, careful not to wake the animals. A Monster Watch had been issued earlier that evening over every Hobble Tube in town, warning the citizens of Hobble to remain inside the town walls until the mysteries had been solved. But Moony only intended to go so far as Town Square.

From the corner of the apothecary shop, he fixed his eyes on the faint aurora rising from the crater outside the Ministry.

Just before Moony approached the meteorite, the front doors of the Museum Of Wonders flung open, and a masked man wearing a frock coat hobbled down the steps, using a cane as his crutch. He seemed to be wearing some kind of burlap sack over his head and hands. The midnight figure also carried a thick, leather-bound book under his arms. Moony watched as the stranger slunk into the shadows behind the museum.

After checking the streets once more to make sure he was alone, Moony approached the giant crater. The same wordless song he had heard while looking out the skylight now called to him, a whispering which conveyed strange and wondrous things he did not altogether understand.

When Moony climbed down into the crater, his entire body became bathed in cosmic light. He recalled the bewildered crowd from earlier that afternoon, and how even the grown men had not been able to move the fallen star. He felt foolish for even trying.

But the meteorite drew him in like a powerful magnet. Wrapping his fingers around the fallen star, he felt its warmth within his callused palms. It was perfectly oval, like an egg, and as smooth as a polished stone.

Moony closed his eyes, and tugged with all his might.

It worked.

As he felt the meteorite detach from the floor of the crater, he stared down at it in bewitched wonder. Moony took a deep breath and for a moment pondered the meaning of his impossible treasure.

He would present the meteorite to Mayor Humplestock the next morning and claim the reward. One hundred tokens would be enough to buy Jezzy the medicine she needed and also to pay C.C. Pottleman for a month's rent at the inn. He would even have enough tokens left over to buy himself the glyder he had long desired.

His grandmother was right—his day of glory had arrived!

Chapter 7:

A Surprise Invitation

Moony ran into the barn, and closed the door. Only when he was safe within his sanctuary of hay and sleeping animals did he dare to unveil his prize from beneath his shirt. Wakened by the otherworldly glow of the stone, the animals stared in confusion upon their caretaker's newfound treasure.

The stable boy swiftly climbed up the ladder into the solitude of his barn loft. He stuffed the meteorite into a nearby hay bale, but its light still emanated throughout the loft.

Moony lay down in his bed, closed his eyes, and imagined the weight of one hundred tokens in his hands.

But just as he rolled over to go to sleep, something poked his side, something which had not been there when he had set out for Town Square half an hour before.

"A letter?" Moony whispered.

He cautiously picked up the black envelope. When he moved it into a stream of moonlight pouring in through the open skylight, six words appeared on the letter's silky, black cover:

An Urgent Message For Moony Jarman

Using his pocketknife, he carefully unsealed the envelope. Inside was a dark leaf of paper, burned along its edges. Moony turned the knob at the base of his lantern, and fed the cloth wick further to create more light. But as he did so, the words on the letter dissolved. When he held the letter back into the moonlight, the message re-appeared. The words were the color of the moonlight itself—a strange, silver ink written in a cursive script.

Wind chimes clanked in the open skylight as Moony quietly read the letter:

> *Dear Moony,*
>
> *The Council Of Moonbloods requests your presence at a secret meeting upon the morrow's witching hour. If you dare accept our invitation, then journey to Hobble's centermost tree at the Clock Tower's third strike. Press the four largest knots of the trunk which cradles Midnight Creek, and an ancient door will open for you. The passageway will lead you to the location of our secret assembly.*
>
> *Bring the Luminary with you, and tell NO ONE you have found it. Your life and the lives of your family are in great danger.*

Moony dropped the letter in the hay and took a deep, trembling breath. A warm tingling electrified his entire body.

Someone had seen him lift the meteorite.

Though he worried about his family, fear and excitement flooded his veins.

Perhaps they will pay me more than one hundred tokens for the meteorite, he thought.

And there, signed at the bottom of the black letter, were eleven signatures, all penned in wet, silver ink. Moony stared at the individual names of the Council Of Moonbloods. He did not recognize the first ten names, but the last one turned Moony cold with terror.

It was the signature of a man he *knew* to be dead:

Happy Gumbledump

Chapter 8:

Into The Tree

Moony's lantern cast a circle of light on the ground as he crossed the East Bridge and crept along the bank of Midnight Creek.

Words from the letter rang in his head: *If you dare accept our invitation, then journey to Hobble's centermost tree at the Clock Tower's third strike.*

Up ahead, through the thick darkness, he saw a tiny, orange ember pulsating next to a giant tree which leaned over the creek.

"That must be the centermost tree in Hobble," Moony whispered into the honeyed night.

As he neared the giant timber, he saw a man smoking a pipe, cradled by the tree's thick, twisting trunk. The stranger stared across the festival field toward the Forbidden Watchtower. Moony wondered if the stranger was waiting for him to arrive, so he could lead him to the Council Of

Moonbloods.

Or was he waiting to ambush him?

After all, the letter had specifically warned of danger, and even death.

Moony pulled himself into the shadows and watched the stranger. After a moment, the old man slowly stood up, knocked the embers of his pipe bowl onto the ground, and ambled across the creek bridge, back toward Town Square.

Moony realized who it was: the curator at the Museum Of Wonders.

Pappy Cricklewood.

Before Moony approached the Center Tree, he waited until the famed war veteran disappeared across the creek bridge.

The tree reminded Moony of a witch. Fluffy moss hung from the tree's branches like strands of grey hair, and the trunk twisted like the wrinkles of an old woman's face.

He easily located the four knots, and found them to be connected in the shape of a diamond.

Moony did as instructed, and a strange grumbling bellowed from deep within the tree. The trunk slid open, and he cautiously stepped into the ancient passageway, planting his lantern into the darkness. As soon as he was inside the belly of the tree, the door rumbled shut behind him.

"Wait!" he yelped.

Moony turned and held the lantern downward, where a pit opened near his feet. He slid down the steep hill of rubble which led to the entrance of a long, dark tunnel. Then he stepped forward, one foot in front of the other, unsure of which direction he was being led.

After walking for what seemed like an eternity, he came upon a laddered wall ahead. Moony set his lantern on the ground and removed the meteorite from beneath his shirt. The fallen star filled the passageway with a cloud of stunning blue light, illuminating stone walls covered with strange paintings.

Moony ascended the ladder, sensing he was near to the secret assembly. But again, he found himself locked in a tree trunk. He groped for some kind of lever to open the door from the inside, but found nothing. As he turned to retrace his journey, he accidentally stepped on a tree root growing through the inner wall of the tree, and a door rumbled open.

Moony gazed out from the tree door in frightful surprise.

There before him, loomed his greatest fear.

Death.

Moaning tombs and crumbling gravestones gazed back at Moony. Shadows snuck over the mossy graves and conjured chills up his spine. He looked out at the Hobble Graveyard, and felt his body tense.

He cautiously stepped out of the tree, and his feet crunched over the fallen leaves.

A chorus of children's laughter echoed through the forest like a dreamy, faraway carnival.

In the distance, Moony saw the bouncing beam of a boxlite slicing through the darkness of the Lostwood, where a dozen children played a forbidden night game. Moony recognized Huff Howler and Hoot Cricklewood amongst them.

"Must be playing Goblinlight," Moony whispered to

himself, wishing he could join them—wishing he had never received the secret invitation from the Moonbloods.

He began creeping through the eerie labyrinth of graves, haunted by the thought that a thousand corpses lay rotting beneath his feet, corpses who were at one time twelve years of age.

Death, Moony mused. *Death is a terrible darkness.*

The stable boy passed by hundreds of gravestones with faded names and remembrances of Hobblers past.

Farther and farther, he walked into the landscape of graves, looking for the members of the mysterious council. But Moony did not know where to look, or even if he had come to the right place. He rubbed the Luminary with his hands, hoping it would reveal some clue.

I never should have come here, Moony thought to himself, as he stood beneath the limbs of a great tree. *It's just me and the Dead tonight.*

Right then, a stream of moonlight crept over the giant timber, and a deep, faraway music began to play in the night.

A ribbon of white mist poured out of the tree trunk and danced into the moonlight as the haunting elegy played.

"It's a ghost," Moony whispered.

Chapter 9:

The Meaning Of Moonblood

A pale phantom materialized in the silver moonlight and stared back at Moony with soft, twinkling eyes. The specter was old, yet moved with youthful fluidity. His long, white hair melted into his foamy beard, and he wore the simple garments of a Hobbler from long ago.

Moony wanted to scream, but his throat felt full of cotton.

"Do not be afraid, boy," the ghost spoke. "I will not harm you. You may consider me a friend."

For a moment, the moonlight faded, and the old ghost dissolved in front of Moony's disbelieving eyes. A thick cloud had swallowed the moon above, transforming the entire graveyard into a sanctuary of darkness. Moony scanned the shadows, wondering where the ghost had vanished.

Suddenly, beams of moonlight again dripped through the trees above, and the phantom reappeared.

The ghost's bare feet floated just above the ground. Moony could see through the transparent form, where the limbs of the trees behind the phantom created the illusion of a skeleton.

"I can only be seen in moonlight," the ghost revealed as he waved his colorless hand, which disappeared and reappeared as it passed in and out of the creamy moonbeam.

"My name is Magi," the ghost introduced himself. "I am the one who invited you here tonight."

Moony attempted to speak, "But you're—you're—"

"A ghost," Magi concluded with a soft chuckle. "I'm dead, Moony. I am no longer alive—at least not in the way you are."

"I don't understand," the boy confessed.

"You see, life and existence are two different things. We ghosts *exist* everywhere—in your houses, sitting at your dinner tables, walking the streets of Town Square. But we must return to the Tree Of The Dead upon every moonrise, lest our existence be revealed to the Living. It is better they do not know we wander beyond the grave," Magi said, smiling down at Moony. "I see you brought the Luminary."

"I only did what the letter asked me to do," Moony replied, hoping the ghost would offer a reward larger than Mayor Humplestock's.

"You should be more careful," Magi warned. "Not every letter you receive will have as noble of intentions as ours. You must always be on your guard."

"Then how do I know I haven't been tricked by *you*?" Moony challenged.

The old ghost chuckled.

"Yes, who's to say? I suppose you must listen to those sharp instincts of yours. What do they tell you?"

"I haven't decided yet," Moony responded. "But how did you know I would be able to lift the meteorite? And how did you send the letter so quickly?"

"The Dead see many things Past, Present, and Future—not *all* things, but many," the ghost explained. "We have always known you would lift the Luminary. The object you carry is not a fallen star as most Hobblers believe it to be. It is something much more powerful." Magi paused, "And much more dangerous. Many would kill to have such power."

"What is it then?" Moony asked, following Magi's gaze down to the pulsating, blue rock.

"It is a gift from some force far more powerful than any Hobbler, dead or living, could ever comprehend," Magi confided. "If you look in the history books of Hobble, you will see that Hobblers have documented many so-called fallen meteorites throughout the centuries—meteorites which always mysteriously disappear."

"Where do they go?" Moony asked, curiously.

"The Protectors find them. Somehow, someway, the Luminary draws them to it," Magi explained.

"The Protector?"

"Yes. Whenever a new Protector is needed, the Light chooses a pure soul to watch over Hobble. But the identity of the Protector is always kept secret from other Hobblers."

Moony was boggled by the idea that such a powerful

person had always secretly existed in the midst of Hobblers.

"So you're the Protector then?" Moony asked, thinking the ghost wanted his special stone back—and that he would pay a hefty price for its safe return.

"I once was," Magi said in a reverent voice. "Now, I am the leader of the Council Of Moonbloods. We are comprised of those who were *once* the chosen Protectors of Hobble—that is, before we died. You will meet the rest of the council in time. For now, they wait inside the Tree Of The Dead."

Moony pondered Magi's words.

"Why are you telling me these things?" the boy questioned.

Magi laughed, and a cloud of sparkling light danced out of the ghost's mouth.

"My boy," Magi said. "I tell you this because *you* are the chosen Protector."

The words pierced through Moony.

"There must be a mistake," Moony replied. "I'm just a stable boy. I can't be the one you're looking for."

"The Light has chosen you because you are best suited to become the Protector at this time," the ghost confirmed. "Just as the Light chose me and the other Moonbloods from our own generations, so it has chosen you. Malivar, our greatest enemy, will soon return. Hobble will be in need of its Protector—in need of you, Moony. Hobble will not survive without you during the Dark Time to come."

Moony looked down at the Luminary, and thought of his responsibilities back at home.

I could save Jezzy's life and pay rent with the one hundred tokens Mayor Humplestock is promising, he thought. *But if I hand over the Luminary to the Moonbloods, I won't have the meteorite to claim the reward back in town.*

Moony looked up at the ghost.

"I thought you invited me to come here tonight because you wanted to buy the stone," Moony confessed. "I thought you might offer a higher price than the Mayor. That's why I came. I'm sorry, but I think you have the wrong Hobbler. You'll have to find someone else to be the Protector."

The ghost sighed, and looked down at Moony with a solemn stare. For a moment, Moony feared the ghost might punish him for his decision.

"I am sorry to hear what you have chosen," Magi said calmly. "I thought—I thought you were the Promised One."

Moony noticed a sorrow in Magi's voice. The ghost seemed disappointed—even broken.

"The Promised One?" Moony questioned.

"Yes, the Jypsis have long prophesied of a Hobbler who would reunite Hobblers with the True Light."

"I'm sorry. But I'm—I'm just a boy. And I'm not the Protector of anything except my family. I have to take care of them before I do anything else. I have to do the work that needs to be done."

Moony stuffed the Luminary in his pocket, then turned and began to walk back through the thicket of graves.

As he disappeared back through the tree door near the graveyard entrance, a smile spread across Magi's face.

The old ghost knew something Moony did not know.

He knew Moony *was* the Promised One.

Chapter 10:

Shadows On The Wall

Early the next morning, Moony awoke to the sound of hushed voices.

A circle of ghoulish shadows stood near the stables below. Moony looked up to the roof, and noticed the final moonbeams of night leaking through holes in the ceiling.

The Moonbloods, Moony thought.

He feared they had come for the Luminary.

Or for him.

He inched toward the edge of the loft and looked down at the shadows in the barn, but could not make out any faces.

"Shh," an old woman's voice warned. "The boy's sleeping. We don't want to wake him."

It was Moony's grandmother! Moony slid away from the edge of the loft and covered his mouth to silence his breathing.

"The Vothlor are already within the walls of Hobble, there's no doubt about it. Malivar must have found a vessel before the Black Candle was extinguished at the end of the Old War—someone who's been living amongst the Hobblers all these years. We all hoped this day would never come, but now it's here," another man spoke. He sounded like Harper Crisp, the new school principal.

"It's a' gettin' too dangerous," a gruff voice followed. Moony was sure it was Nubb Plotterdub, the town weaponsmith. "Let the Hobblers take care of themselves. We've done our part twice over, and we can't look after 'em forever. It's time we go back to our own people, where we belong."

Moony wondered what Nubb meant by "our own people".

Another voice spoke out, "We could lose our lives. I have a family to take care of. I can't be dying for no Hobblers."

Moony recognized it to be the voice of Dusty Bludpie, the junkyard operator.

The stable boy wondered why the random group had gathered in the barn, and why they were meeting in secret. Nothing made sense—especially his grandmother's presence. Moony lay perfectly still, careful not to draw attention to himself.

"You dare suggest that we flee, but forget why we were sent here in the first place. To watch over the Hobblers. At all costs. Gem and Beatrice are having difficult financial times, but they're still devoted to the cause, even with Pottleman's constant hustling for their rent payments," Principal Crisp challenged. "We cannot tuck our tails and run. We must do what is right, not necessarily what is easy. Besides, if the Vothlor have returned, we'd be in just as much danger back home with our own people as we are here."

There was silence.

Suddenly, another voice addressed the troubled gathering. It was the voice of a little boy, younger than Moony.

"One of the last things my Pa said to me before I came to Hobble was that the Promised One would be coming soon. He said not to lose heart."

Moony heard a fist pound against a tin milking pail.

"Ain't no such thing as the Promised One," Nubb insisted. "It's naught but a pixie tale for boys like yourself to keep hope alive. We've gotta take care of ourselves and not be waitin' around for a savior. Best thing we can do for Hobble is to let the town fall!"

"Ain't gonna help us to be at war with each other," Gem interrupted. "There's dark things at work in Hobble. That much we know to be true. The sun'll be up in half an hour, and we need to be back at our posts before the Hobblers are out and about in town."

Moony was confused as to why his grandmother spoke of Hobblers as if she were not one of them. When the meeting came to an abrupt end, Moony watched their shadows move along the far wall. Each of the conspirators disappeared out of the barn, one by one.

Suddenly, a rooster crowed from below.

Moony sat up and peered at the Luminary glowing from the hay bale next to his bed.

I'm the son of an innkeeper. I clean stables and look after travelers' horses. I can't save Hobble from those . . . things. How could I be the Promised One?

On the way to Town Hall, Moony heard folks buzzing about the missing meteorite.

"It's disappeared! 'Twas here last night, and now it's gone!" Fink Karbunkle explained to the crowd that had gathered around the empty crater.

Moony smiled to himself. He looked into the knapsack he carried and grinned at the glowing blue stone within.

Grown men will admire me, because I did something they couldn't do, he thought.

Just then, Sheriff and Deputy brushed past Moony, followed by a mob of frantic parents.

" . . .Yes, that's right. Hoot Cricklewood and eleven others," Deputy explained to Sheriff, who raced toward Town Hall to inform Mayor Humplestock of the new troubles. "They snuck into the Lostwood to play Goblinlight late last night and never returned. It's the talk of the town, Sheriff. Folks think they're— well—they think the kids might have been killed, like Happy and Guffy. Like all those kids during the Old War."

Moony's stomach churned as he watched the panicked mothers and fathers climb the steps of Town Hall and funnel through the doorway in search of the newly-appointed Mayor.

Moony recalled the laughter of Huff and the other children in the Lostwood the night before. He pictured the bouncing beam of light, and the silhouettes of the playful gamers. Next, images of Red Crisp, the gatekeepers, Mayor Waddletub, and Jezzy flashed through his mind.

Moony suddenly felt a cold, airy presence brush against his neck.

—

He turned around, but no one was near.

Moony opened the knapsack one more time. As he peered down at the secret treasure, he again heard the strange song of his destiny singing within.

And after weighing the possibilities, Moony made a new wager.

Chapter 11:

Ceremony Of Ghosts

Late that night, Moony returned to the graveyard with the Luminary hidden beneath his shirt.

As he walked through the haunted world of tombs and shadows, owls hooted from treetops, crickets chanted in cryptic rhythms, and spiders weaved their webs between waving tree limbs.

Moony crept through the maze of graves, and reverently approached the Tree Of The Dead.

He placed his hand on the ancient tree and gripped its rugged trunk. The tree's giant roots weaved in and out of the ground like stitches in a blanket, disappearing into the world of dead bodies below.

"Hello?" Moony whispered to the tree. "Magi? Can you hear me?"

But there was no answer.

Still, Moony continued, "I came back, and I brought the Luminary with me. I've decided—I've decided to become the Protector."

Suddenly, a silky stream of moonlight spilled through the mossy branches above. The Tree Of The Dead moaned with a thousand tortured voices.

Moony took a step back and waited. The bark of the tree began to glow with a cold, white fire as a carnival of ghosts poured out of its trunk.

One by one, the ghosts leaked into the graveyard and formed a perfect circle around the boy.

Moony gripped the Luminary as he stared at the pale faces of the Council Of Moonbloods. The ghosts were all different ages, from boys not much older than himself to decrepit old men. But each of the Moonbloods possessed a countenance of strength and bravery.

Except for one.

Happy Gumbledump looked as bumbling in death as he had been in life, and Moony wondered how the clumsy gatekeeper had become part of such an elite fraternity of spirits. Happy flung the tail of his stocking cap over his shoulder and waved excitedly at Moony from the circle of phantoms. The gatekeeper's missing eye was now there, as normal as it had been before his boyhood accident.

Perhaps Death heals the wounds of Life, Moony thought.

Moony nodded at the old man in disbelief. Only a few nights before, he had held Happy's bloody head in his hands.

He now knew Happy's secret.

Happy had been the most recent Protector of Hobble.

Finally, the eleventh ghost poured out of the white fire,

and all the ghosts turned and faced Moony.

Magi hovered through the still night air and smiled down at Moony.

"I see you found your way back," he affirmed.

Moony stepped forward and held out the Luminary in his cupped hands.

"Yes, I've changed my mind. I want to become the Protector, if it's not too late."

"Why the change of heart?" Magi questioned.

"Well, I've been thinking about all the awful things happening in Hobble. First, the gatekeepers were murdered," Moony said, glancing at Happy's smiling ghost. "Then Mayor Waddletub vanished. And now over a dozen kids are missing from town. I believe in what you said about the Vothlor coming. Helping Hobble is more important than looking after only my family. Hobble is my family too. *This* is the work that needs to be done."

"It's something you are *destined* to do," Magi assured. "But you must know, there is much responsibility and danger you accept by becoming the Protector. Many things will change in your life, Moony. Once you become the Protector, you cannot tell anyone of your secret identity. You must protect it at all costs. Even death." Magi paused, then added, "You are accepting your death by accepting this destiny, Moony. All Protectors must die for Hobble."

Moony looked down at the countless rows of tombstones and took a step backwards. He did not want to die. He wanted to live a long life and grow to be an old man.

"Does that mean I will die young?" Moony asked.

"Not necessarily," Magi answered. "But in a way, you

will die here tonight. You will sacrifice your own desires for a greater destiny, and you will be reborn unto a new path."

"What will happen to my family? I can't just turn my back on them," Moony resolved, feeling selfish for leaving them to fend for themselves. "I won't do that. They—"

"They will be better off with you as the Protector, as will every other Hobbler."

Moony looked up into Magi's wise, hollow eyes, comforted by the words.

Magi continued, "But no one—not even your family—can ever know your secret. It's a lonely path you must walk, Moony. You are taking on the weight of all Hobblers by accepting this destiny. You will be a savior to them, but they will never know it is you who have saved them. If you can live without glory, and die without being honored, then you are capable of carrying this responsibility."

Moony weighed the possibilities of his future. Part of him wanted to live a simple life and to someday have a family of his own. But he had always known in his heart he was made for a different fate.

"Do you accept this responsibility for all of time?" Magi asked.

"I—I accept it," Moony replied.

Magi smiled, then nodded his head at the other ghosts. The spectrum of Moonbloods tightened their circle around the boy.

"Then you must kneel," Magi instructed.

Moony looked around at the circle of phantoms, and followed the old ghost's instruction. He knelt at the center of the ghost circle, holding the Luminary just above his head like an offering to the moon.

As soon as his knees touched the ground, the other eleven ghosts knelt around him, too. Moony understood the sacred meaning of this action—all Moonbloods humbled themselves before one another.

Magi reached through the calm night air, and touched the glowing, blue Luminary with his misty fingertip.

The Luminary floated out of Moony's palms and hovered in mid-air like a floating star. It grew brighter and smaller, and then it began to sing a deafening tune.

Suddenly, the floating stone zoomed through the air and bored into Moony's chest, lifting him so that he hovered in the center of the ghost circle. The boy opened his mouth to shriek in pain, but suddenly realized the pain had melted away.

Only courage and strength surged through him.

The Luminary glowed within his chest, as if it were a blue heart. Rivers of blue light trailed through his veins, running down his arms and fingertips, expanding out from the Luminary like the branches of a tree. Bright rings of light radiated over the kneeling Moonbloods.

Moony looked up at Magi, and the old ghost's face was calm, as if to assure Moony it was a normal part of the transformation from Hobbler to Moonblood.

"The moon crystals will settle in a moment," Magi assured. "You are transforming into a Moonblood. You are becoming a new creature, Moony."

When it was over, the tree of light within Moony dimmed, and his skin returned to its normal color.

"The Luminary is your new heart. You are the Protector for as long as you choose to walk the Path," Magi confirmed. "Or for as long as the Path allows you to walk it."

All the Moonbloods placed their translucent hands on the boy, and he shivered at the chill of their touch.

"Your next task is to visit the Protector's Sanctuary. No harm or evil can ever touch you there. You will find it northwest of Hobble, twelve miles west of the Light Mines." Magi paused, then added, "Look for the tree which you cannot see."

"But how will I find it if I cannot see it?" Moony asked.

Suddenly, an abyss of clouds began to drift in front of the moon, and the circle of ghosts began to dissolve.

Magi noticed his own fading existence, and quickly instructed, "Look in the hollow of the Tree Of The Dead. Follow the coordinates, and you will find the Protector's Sanctuary. But beware, Moony. The terrors of the Vothlor have only just begun. Your journey will be full of many dangers. Many dangers, indeed . . ."

The old ghost's voice trailed off into a whisper and extinguished like a candle's flame.

"What if—" Moony called after Magi.

But it was too late.

The new Protector reached his hand into the hollow of the Tree Of The Dead, and lifted out a bronze compass.

Chapter 12:

The Strange Brew

As soon as Moony finished sweeping and waxing the floor of the inn the next afternoon, he checked to make sure the compass was still in his trousers pocket, then hurried out the swinging doors.

He crossed through Town Square, and saw a line of children curling out of Plumb's bakery. As he approached the purple door at the front of the bakery, he noticed the new sign that hung above the porch.

Gubbles' Goodies?

"Hey you!" a nasally voice shouted at Moony. "You have to wait at the end of the line like everyone else!"

Moony turned and saw a boy as skinny as a noodle staring back at him though a pair of cracked glasses. The boy wore a skunk-tail cap, and clenched his fists, as if preparing to fight for his place in line.

"I'm not buying anything," Moony explained, puzzled by the ravenous look in the boy's eyes. "I just need to tell Plumb something."

Moony stepped into the cozy bakery, and was overwhelmed by the tantalizing scents of banana pudding, sugar cookies, and chocolate cupcakes cooling in pans scattered across the countertops. Glass jars of peanut-butter cookies and cinnamon stix were displayed on the giant windowsill next to the front door, inviting all Hobblers to come inside the factory of treats.

The newly-painted blue, yellow, and red planks on the floor matched the colors of the dresses worn by the three women who stood behind the bakery counter, greeting each child with alluring smiles.

The woman wearing a dress the color of bluebonnets noticed Moony standing apart from the others in line.

She called out to him, "You there! Couldn't wait in line with the rest, I see." She paused and leaned over the counter to examine Moony from head to toe. Then she whispered softly, "My name is Issa Gubble. And I know just the thing for a boy like you."

The beautiful woman took a wooden spoon from the front pocket of her apron and dipped it into a bubbling cauldron. She then lifted the spoon from the brew, walked around the counter, and offered it to Moony.

"No thanks," Moony said, politely. "I was just looking for Plumb. I wanted to thank her for baking my birthday cake."

The sparkle in the woman's eyes dimmed.

"Our Aunty Plumb is sick in bed," Issa quickly replied. "She's contagious, so we can't allow any visitors. But she would want you to have a taste or two of the new brew."

Issa lifted the spoon up to Moony's lips.

"No thank you. I haven't been feeling very hungry today," Moony said.

"You're a stubborn boy," the woman replied as she glared down at Moony. "Quit making excuses, and drink up."

"Not today, but thank you, Miss Gubble. I best be going now."

"Very well," Issa surrendered. "Another time then!"

She offered the spoonful of brew to the skinny boy wearing the skunk-tail cap. The boy gulped it down, and immediately begged for another.

Moony took a step back and observed the chaotic madness of the bakery. Children were piling toward the wooden counter like wild animals, jumping at each spoonful the Gubble sisters offered. Again and again, the crazed kiddies leapt toward the never-ending 'free tastes' of the brew.

Moony noticed that Issa had wrapped her arm around the skinny boy's shoulders and was guiding him behind the counter and toward the door to the cellar.

Issa opened the door, and led the boy into the pitch black chamber. A moment later, she returned. Alone.

She glanced around the chaotic shop, and smiled innocently at Moony, who watched her with a suspicious glare.

"Ready for a taste?" Issa offered, playfully raising her eyebrows.

Moony approached the counter and asked, "Where did that boy go?"

"What boy?" Issa questioned.

"The boy you just took into the cellar," Moony accused. "Where is he?"

"We don't have a cellar," Issa replied, astonished by the question.

"But I just saw you take him there with my own eyes."

Issa leaned over the countertop, smiled, and said, "Your eyes are playing tricks on you, boy. I've heard a few children complaining about nightmares as of late, and maybe you're having one now. No children are allowed behind the counter, except on special occasions. Now please excuse me. I have hungry customers to attend to."

Moony felt the Luminary pulse within his chest.

Seeing that the Gubble sisters were distracted by the clamor of eager tasters, he snuck around the side of the counter and crept toward the cellar door. But when he looked inside, it was empty.

Moony turned around, only to meet the twisted grimace of Issa Gubble. Veins bulged in her hands as she gripped the wooden spoon and shook it at Moony's face.

"Foolish boy!" Issa threatened as she grabbed Moony's arm. "I already told you that your eyes are playing tricks on you, and they're going to get you into a heap of trouble!"

"I—I had to see it for myself," Moony replied, wondering if his eyes *had* played tricks on him after all.

"Come back when you're ready for a free taste," Issa commanded. "Until then, stay away from here. A nosy boy is a naughty boy!"

She dragged Moony around the counter, through the gathering of children, and shoved him out the front door.

As Moony walked down the bakery's steps, he reached

—
54

into his pocket and lightly touched the Protector's compass. He then looked back over his shoulder through the bakery window at the three giggly sisters feeding the swarm of drooling children with their strange brew.

The Luminary burned hot in his chest.

It told him that the Gubble sisters had a secret. A dark secret.

Chapter 13:

The Tree That Wasn't There

Twilight hues of deep purple and blue spread across the Hobble sky, but beneath the canopy of the Lostwood, it was always as dark as midnight.

Moony rode his bay horse through the haunted woods, gripping the lantern he had brought from the stable. A comforting glow encircled him, casting brief shadows upon the trunks of giant, thorn-colored trees and the forest's leafy floor. Moony rubbed his thumb over the glass face of the compass, and headed northwest toward the Protector's Sanctuary.

Why had the Moonbloods built the sanctuary so far from Hobble? he wondered.

Like most Hobblers, Moony had never before set foot in the northern Lostwood. Nearly all of the battlefields of the Old War lay in the southern forests.

Up ahead, Moony saw an opening, and galloped

through the crooked archway of trees, stopping next to a lake, where twinkling waters reflected the rising, orange moon.

Across the way, two shimmering waterfalls poured off steep cliffs.

Moony dismounted his horse, and led her by the reins around the edge of the pond to the base of a stone stairwell, which ascended beside the left waterfall. The horse whinnied in fright and jerked the reins out of Moony's hand. Moony tried to calm the bay, but she ran back into the Lostwood from whence they had come.

She's smart enough to find her way back home, Moony thought, hoping his own sense of direction was as good as the mare's.

He turned and looked down at the compass coordinates, which pointed to somewhere above the stone stairwell. Beads of water sprayed off the waterfall and tickled Moony's face as he climbed the damp, crumbling steps. The stairwell rose a hundred feet up.

When Moony arrived at the top of the steps, he discovered the source of the twin waterfalls—a wild, rushing river the color of the moon. The river was split at the cliff's edge by a giant boulder, which formed the two separate falls. Moony crept along the riverbank, trusting the compass coordinates, but could not find any sign of the Protector's Sanctuary.

He shook his compass to make sure it was working. The needle beneath the dusty glass face pointed directly in front of him, toward the middle of the river.

Moony recalled Magi's last words, *"Look for the tree which you cannot see."*

Moony peered into the raging waters.

If I walk too far into the river, I'll be cast over the edge of the cliffs, he thought.

Moony removed his soggy boots, and rolled his pants cuffs up to his knees. He lifted the hissing lantern up high and trudged out into the cold, slow-moving shallows, stopping just before the flow of the river turned wild.

According to the compass's needle, the Protector's Sanctuary was only a few feet in front of him.

It has to be underwater, Moony decided.

He closed his eyes and held tight to his lantern. Then he stuffed the bronze compass into his trousers pocket, held his breath, and dove beneath the treacherous waters.

He frantically felt for a hidden door or a secret passageway beneath the river's surface.

But there was nothing there.

Only the wildness of the river.

Instantly, the water wrapped around Moony and dragged him toward the edge of the cliff.

Chapter 14:

Behind The Waterfalls

Moony clawed at the furious waters, searching for something, anything, to stop himself from being sucked beneath the rapids.

I'm going to die, he thought. *And no one will ever find my body.*

Suddenly, Moony's hand gripped onto something hard. He clung to the object, and held himself in place while the river tugged against his shoulders. The rushing water ripped Moony's lantern out of his hand and quickly carried it over the edge of the falls. He looked up, hoping to climb out of the undercurrent, but flinched in fright at the massive monster looming above him.

Only, it was not a monster at all, but a tree—an enormous, magnificent, otherworldly tree.

It had not been there a moment before, but his touch now allowed him to see it. The tree's thick, wild branches canopied over the river from bank to bank, and towered high above the giant timbers of the surrounding Lostwood. It was the most incredible thing Moony had ever seen.

Right then, the knotted tail of a rope lowered next to Moony.

"Grab hold!" a voice called from above.

Moony grabbed the rope and climbed it one knot at a time.

On the first limb of the tree was a platform. Struggling to catch his breath, Moony heaved himself onto it, and huffed for air. When he looked up, he was dazzled by the fantastical world around him. The giant treehouse seemed to go on forever. Candles flickered upon every limb like fallen stars stuck to the tree's branches, and lanterns dangled from dozens of fish hooks tied to noosed twines. Moony stood to his feet and gazed around, awestruck.

"Been expectin' ya'!" a jolly voice chimed.

Moony looked down and saw a man who stood about waist-high. The stranger wore cut-off trousers made of rabbit skins, ornamented with leaves and twigs. A deerskin jacket wrapped around his shoulders and covered his bare, silver-haired chest.

"Just in time for dinner," the dwarf said, as if he had known Moony his entire life.

The little man carried a bucket of fresh catfish and lifted it up to show Moony his success.

"Gimble's my name. And I know who you are. O yessiree!, I know who you are. Been waitin' for you a long time now, in fact."

Gimble walked past Moony and motioned for the boy to follow.

—

60

Moony stared at the little man, whose white beard flowed down to his feet like a miniature waterfall.

"Are—are you one of the Moonbloods?" Moony asked.

"Ha!" the man laughed. "There ain't enough buried treasures in all the Lostwood to make me want that job. A frightful path, it is."

Gimble led Moony up a bamboo staircase lined with jars of fireflies. "I'm the keeper of the house, so to speak," he continued. "I cook when you need eatin', clean when you make a mess, and listen when you need a talkin'. Otherwise, I'll be out of your way. Solitude's a man's best friend, and you'll have plenty of it here. But if ever you need me, I'm only a shout away."

They arrived at the highest floor of the tree house and walked down a twinkling hallway bathed with warm, colorful light. A long line of stained-glass windows covered the walls. Night had fallen, and starlight illuminated the gallery of windows, awakening the glass to its intended glory.

Moony admired the brilliant scenes depicted upon the windowpanes.

"Who are they?" Moony asked, referring to the warriors shown in the scenes on the windows.

"Protectors of the past," Gimble revealed. "Dearest of friends, they are. When your curiosities lead you, you may speak a name into each window, and the scene will move for you. The windows tell their stories."

Moony wondered if his own story would one day be immortalized upon one of the windows.

I must live a good story, Moony told himself. *A legend worth remembering.*

They climbed into a cozy hollow where a cast-iron cauldron hung in a hearth. Moony took a seat at the tree-stump table, where he watched Gimble fidget with pots and pans. The little man ladled a heaping portion of fish stew into a clay bowl.

"Give that a try, and tell me it ain't the best thing to ever touch yer lips," Gimble said, placing the bowl in front of Moony.

Gimble's pride in his cooking was well-founded. After feasting on the stew, Gimble stood up from his stool, belched, and motioned for Moony to follow him. He led the boy through a curving corridor until they arrived at an opening in the main trunk of the treehouse.

"There," Gimble pointed at the dark hollow. He handed Moony a lantern and explained, "The Trunkslide will take you where you need to go. I believe Magi left something for you."

Moony observed the opening in the tree and turned back to the little man. "Magi? Is he here?"

But Gimble was already walking away.

Moony cautiously sat on the ledge of the hollow's opening, and pushed himself into the tunnel, guided by the lantern's flickering glow. His stomach dropped as he slid down the steep slide, spiraling through the thick trunk, until he finally landed in a pool of cold water far below.

After crawling up onto a rocky bank, he looked around and suddenly realized he was *behind* the twin waterfalls.

The roaring falls poured over the eyes of the cave, where fireflies played October games in the chilly spray. A giant rock stood between the two waterfalls, making the openings of the cave look like the eye sockets of a skull.

Twelve unlit torches hung upon the mossy walls of the lair, all exactly twelve feet apart from one another.

A small, wooden table sat between the two middlemost torches, and upon it was an unfurled yellowed scroll.

Moony approached the table, and read its calligraphic message:

> *Moony,*
>
> *It is time for you to acquire your first power. Every Protector is allowed twelve during his or her legacy. But you must only request a power from the Luminary when it is vital to your task. Do not waste your choices. You may only receive one power during each October. When a time arises and you need supernatural assistance, simply close your eyes and focus upon the ability you desire. The Luminary will do the rest.*
>
> *But beware...*
>
> *With each power comes much pain.*
>
> *-Magi*

Moony lowered the scroll from the moonlight and turned back toward the waterfall. Then he gazed out into the foamy waters, contemplating the scroll's promises. He closed his eyes, just as the scroll had instructed told him to do.

I wish I could fly. I wish I could fly. I wish. . .

Suddenly, Moony's chest began to glow in the darkness. The Luminary pulsed beneath his skin.

A burning sensation pinched the top of his spine—like a thousand hot needles digging into his flesh.

Chapter 15:

Mooncradled

As the pain pierced into Moony's spine, he cocked his head back in agony and collapsed to his knees.

Seeking relief, he crawled forward to the pool of icy water and dove in, but the tortuous sensation continued to grow. Moony let out a scream, which rattled the very rocks of the cave. Steam poured off his scalded back, and the arid scent of scorched flesh loitered in the musty air.

Finally, the pain dimmed.

Moony examined the crest of his spine with trembling fingertips, but felt no blood or wound.

No scar.

Nothing.

Right then, one of the twelve torches on the wall erupted into flame and revealed a mirror speckled with

---

grime and hidden amongst a thicket of vines.

Moony blinked in astonishment, wondering how the torch had come to life on its own. He walked over to the mirror. A mottled reflection stared back at him. He pulled his soaking wet shirt over his head and examined his tingling spine in the sooty reflection.

There, just below his neck, he saw a strange, black symbol.

The tattoo was an emblem of the very power he had spoken to the Luminary.

A pair of wings.

Moony climbed up the giant rock which curled over the edge of the shallow pool. After taking in a deep breath, he leapt from the stone, but felt himself only falling toward the shallow pool below.

He quickly spread his arms to break his fall, and felt a surge of energy rush through his veins and spread throughout his entire body. The moon crystals tingled beneath his flesh.

Just before he would have nosedived into the pool, Moony shot through the waterfalls like an arrow, and flew out over the Lostwood. Within a moment, the Protector's Sanctuary seemed a world away as he soared above the forest pond.

He was flying! Flying! Flying! Flying!

A blanket of stars spread out above him in the deepening night. He felt in complete control of his body, unafraid of the expanse of sky above and the water below.

Moony swooshed downward and skimmed over the surface of the pond, dipping his finger into the still, dark water and cutting it like butter. He soared up into the

October night like a crazed firefly, flipping a dozen times, each time with a cheer of wild elation. The entire forest seemed to be watching as he ascended deeper into the sea of stars above, ornamented by the rising moon.

He laughed like a madman at the pure elation of it.

How can this be?! Moony wondered. *Only yesterday I was sweeping filthy floors. Now I'm flying!*

High above Hobble, the quiet town looked like a tiny dollhouse—just a tiny speck of twinkling existence in the vastness of the dark Lostwood. Even the Candletin Inn seemed a world away, though Moony knew he could soar down to the front porch in no time at all.

Next, he darted west toward the Mountain Of Light, where miners harvested raw coals of Light.

Far below, he saw several dozen miners scavenging along the side of the mountain. The men scaled up the train cars and removed heavy black bags, then quickly dragged the bags into the tunnels of the mountain.

Seems strange for the miners to be working in the middle of the night, Moony thought.

He was about to fly down for a closer look, when he heard a whooshing sound in the sky behind him. Instead, he descended into the forest, and perched in the treetops.

Three dark shadows flew across the sky directly above him, headed toward the mines. Moony could not tell if they were giant birds or flying monsters, but was certain he had seen the tails of…

three broomsticks.

Chapter 16:

Exchange Of Riches

The next morning, Moony awoke just before sunrise. He lay in bed with his eyes closed, and listened to the scratchy sound of milk spraying into a tin pail in the stables below.

Jezzy must be feeling better if she's well enough to do her morning chores, Moony thought, relieved his sister was back to her normal self.

Suddenly, the rapid milking stopped, and Moony heard footsteps crunch across the hay-covered floor—footsteps too heavy to be Jezzy's.

He quickly turned over and looked through the knothole in the floor of the loft.

His grandmother stood in the barn below.

She bent down and picked up a shiny, black letter from the ground.

The Moonblood letter.

The last minutes of morning twilight still lingered, and a gentle, creamy ray of moonlight poured in through the open skylight, illuminating the center of the barn. Gem held the letter into the ray of moonlight, and silver words appeared on the page.

"Oh my stars . . ." Gem whispered.

Moony jumped from the loft and flew down behind Gem.

"Mornin' Grammy," Moony said, now standing right behind his grandmother.

The old woman jumped two feet in the air and kicked over the pail of fresh milk.

"Where'd you come from, boy? You can't sneak up on an old woman like that!"

Moony searched for an explanation, "I—I just got in. From a morning walk."

Gem looked up at the barn loft, suspiciously, then back at Moony. She squinted her eyes.

"I could've sworn I heard you snoring up there. Anyhow, I was just milking the cows for Jezzy. Poor thing. She's still feeling rotten as an egg."

"No better than yesterday?" Moony asked.

Gem solemnly shook her head. "I hate to think what might happen to her, Moony. What this family needs is a miracle, or else we'll lose the Candletin. And maybe even Jezzy."

Moony's heart ached. He felt a stab of regret, wondering if he should have followed his first instinct to turn the meteorite in to the mayor. If he had claimed the one hundred tokens, his family would have had all of their needs met.

Moony quickly snatched the Moonblood letter out of Gem's hand.

"Thanks for finding this, Grammy. Must have fallen from the loft," he said and walked past his grandmother.

"Better keep your valuables in a safer place," Gem called after Moony, but he had already disappeared out the door.

Later that morning, Moony was still unsure if he had made the right decision. As he polished the tabletops of the inn, he feared that Jezzy would die because of his choice. After all, he had possessed something valuable, but had chosen to keep it for himself.

His thoughts were soon interrupted by two men discussing the latest news of Hobble over a pitcher of warm cider.

"Some say it was Winky Waddletub who moved the meteorite, others say it was the Vothlor. Director Stevens says it was Crump Critchfield, and Zappy Fizzler says it was Happy and Guffy from beyond the grave."

The man spoke in fierce, deep whispers. When he turned his head, Moony noticed an old scar across the brow of the man's left eye. It was the same Outskirter who had tested Moony on the night of the Star Festival by dropping a mug from the table.

Tog Gockle, manager of the Light Dock, sat across the table from the mysterious Outskirter, and boisterously replied, "They're all blasted theories, Patchfoot. Truth is, no one knows what happened to it. Simple as that." Tog stood and put on his tricorn hat. "I've gotta be going.

We've got a big shipment going out—I mean—*coming in* this morning. This October's been busier than ever."

Moony immediately remembered what he had seen the night before near the Mountain Of Light. The miners had unloaded dozens of black bags from the train and carried them into the mountain. Moony wondered what they were shipping *out* of Hobble.

Patchfoot lifted his mug, and bid farewell to Tog, who quickly exited out the door.

The Outskirter then turned to Moony and asked, "What do you think about the missing meteorite, boy?"

Moony began nervously sweeping the floor.

"I—I didn't move it. I don't know who did," he replied.

"No one said *you* moved it. Why so nervous, boy?" Patchfoot questioned, eyeing Moony.

Just then, a customer in the corner of the room stood from his table. The stranger was seven feet tall and wore a brown, hooded cloak which hid his face. Moony could not help but notice the man's coal-black teeth—black as the pebbles in Midnight Creek.

The giant approached Moony, covering the boy with his shadow.

"For your services," the man said in a rugged voice. The customer flicked a gold coin, which sang through the air and landed in Moony's callused palm.

"Thank you, sir," Moony replied.

Moony watched through the windows as the stranger climbed onto the perch of his black stagecoach, which was outfitted with a team of four black stallions and a purple lantern. The man soon started a conversation with the new town paperboy, Notch Cricklewood, and flicked him a similar coin in exchange for a copy of the *Hobble Gazette*.

Patchfoot eyed the giant as he walked out the door.

"Strange," the Outskirter mumbled to himself. "That looked just like—ah, but it can't be."

He quickly turned to Moony.

"Lemme see that coin." The Outskirter's eyes widened as he gazed into Moony's palm. "That's—that's a Topkins coin! Didn't think any of these were still around. It's worth at least a hundred tokens."

Patchfoot smiled and placed his hand on Moony's shoulder.

"Say, boy, I'll give you a hundred tokens for this coin. It ain't gonna do you much good now. Hobblers switched from gold coins to tokens fifty years ago. But I'm a collector of sorts, and I'll pay you full price for it."

Patchfoot held up a burlap sack full of tokens. Moony thought it strange for the man to have so many tokens on hand, but Outskirters often came to town to purchase several months worth of supplies.

"Sounds like a fair exchange," Moony replied, trying to hide his excitement.

He handed Patchfoot the Topkins coin, and Patchfoot handed Moony the sack of one hundred tokens. They smiled at one another, both satisfied with their exchange. Patchfoot then shook Moony's hand and hurried out the door of the inn.

Moony smiled upon the sack of tokens. It was the exact amount he would have received for turning in the meteorite to Mayor Humplestock. Fortune had fallen in his favor. He now had enough tokens to pay rent and to buy Jezzy the medicine she needed.

Perhaps I made the right decision after all, Moony exulted.

Chapter 17:

Promise Of Nostrum

Moony hurried into Town Square, holding his bag of tokens close to his chest.

He smiled, thinking about how excited Jezzy would be when he brought her the apothecary's strongest nostrum. But on the way to the Apothecary's Shop, Moony saw something which caught his attention.

A long line of kids poured into Gubbles' Goodies—a line twice as long as it had been the day before. Tubb Wiggins, Mayor Waddletub's grandson, pushed his way through the door of the bakery, licking his lips and waving his arms in excitement. Several other kids followed in Tubb's wake.

And there, at the very back of the line, was a little girl in a silky, pink nightgown.

"Jezzy!" Moony shouted. "Jezzy, what are you doing here? You're supposed to be in bed!"

Moony rushed to the back of the line and squatted next to his little sister. He turned his back on the boy sitting in an electro-wagon—a boy wearing a white laboratory coat and green-lensed goggles. Moony then noticed a few sprinkles of blood scattered on Jezzy's mittens where she had been coughing.

Jezzy looked up at Moony with her soft, brown eyes, and confessed, "I couldn't help it, Moony. I smelled the scent through my window. I—I wanted just one free taste."

Moony feared the craving in Jezzy's eyes.

He warned his sister, "You stay away from here, understand? There's something strange about the Gubbles. I don't trust them. Go home, and stay in bed! I don't want to see you back here ever again."

Jezzy looked at the bakery door one last time, then nodded her head in reluctant obedience.

Moony squinted his eyes, concerned at Jezzy's desire for the brew, and pressed his hand against her forehead.

"You're hot as a fire," he said. "Fever's getting worse."

Moony touched the side of his sister's flushed face and smiled, "Go on back to the inn, so we can get you feeling better. I have enough tokens to buy the apothecary's best nostrum now. You'll be better in no time. Everything is going to be alright now."

He held up his bag of tokens and jingled them 'til she smiled.

"I feel good enough to go with you," Jezzy said with a smile. "Unless you're worried about me going to the apothecary too."

Just then, the Light Train whistled in the distance.

Burd Trubbles brushed the tail of her broomstick against the wood-planked floor of her potions shop.

The old woman's frizzled, white hair danced in the air as she chugged her body back and forth with each sweep. Her two egg-white eyes sat like twin moons amidst the wrinkled constellation of her face.

Her mouth curled into a toothless crescent-smile at the sound of footsteps entering her shop.

Moony held Jezzy's hand as they wound through the wondrous emporium. Cages of tiny animals hung from the ceiling rafters, ingredients for potions and nostrums glimmered in glass jars, and black cats coiled upon every table. Moony was awed by the bottles stacked upon the cobwebbed shelves from floor to ceiling: sleep potions, love potions, strength potions, healing potions. The choices were as endless as the stars.

"What can I do for you two young Hobblers?" Burd asked, staring directly at Moony.

He peered back into the old frump's milky eyes, wondering how she could follow his every move with such precision.

"Just because I'm blind doesn't mean I can't see," Burd chirped with a witchy chuckle, sensing Moony's thoughts. "Now, what might you be looking for today?"

Right then, Jezzy coughed, and Moony wrapped his arm around her frail shoulder.

"My sister's been sick for weeks, but we haven't had enough tokens to buy her medicine 'til now. We need something strong and quick. Her fever is getting worse every day."

The old woman set her broomstick against the counter, and replied, "Why didn't you come to me sooner, boy? Burd Trubbles would never let a child suffer."

Burd climbed up a ladder to the top shelf behind the service counter. She sniffed along the long rack of potions until she stopped at a potent scent.

"Rosemary roots and crickets' teeth," she warbled, then stepped down the ladder and handed the tiny glass bottle to Moony.

It felt warm, like a bottled ember.

He reached into his bag of tokens.

"There'll be no charge today, young man. I understand hard times, and I know ol' Pottleman is hounding your momma. I only wish you'd a come to me sooner. Have her take four spoonfuls tonight and three in the morning. Two at a time after that, until she's back to normal."

"Thank you, Miss Trubbles. We won't forget your kindness," Moony said gratefully. He took Jezzy's hand and quickly led her back through the warren of cats and cages, toward the front door of the apothecary shop.

Jezzy had already stepped outside when Burd called after Moony.

"Wait a minute, boy."

Moony turned around to look at the old woman, whose tattered rags of clothing fluttered in the faint breeze.

"Come here. Come close," she called, waving her hand.

Moony slowly walked toward the apothecary.

"Closer, closer," she whispered, until Moony stood only inches in front of her.

She reached out her skeletal hands and wrapped them around the boy's face. Her pale eyes bored into Moony's.

"I sense it in you," she whispered.

Moony felt the room grow colder.

"What do you sense?" he asked. He tried to pull free from the old woman's hands, but they gripped his face like a vice.

The apothecary blinked her eyes and whispered, "Death. It's already written your name in its book. I see Malivar in your path. Beware of every step you take, boy. Find a way to protect yourself, and never turn a blind eye to the Darkness, lest you find yourself in the grave. I've seen the vision."

Chapter 18:

A Serendipitous Choice

After Moony took Jezzy back to the inn and served her four spoonfuls of the nostrum, he took his bag of tokens and returned to Town Square.

Just outside the Ministry, he ran into Notch Cricklewood.

"Sorry to hear about your little brother," Moony said, imagining what it would be like to lose Jezzy.

"Thanks," Notch replied. "My Pappy says Hoot and Red and the others are probably just lost in the woods. Says they'll be back soon. Sort of strange being some of the last kids left in town though. It's only you and me and a couple dozen others left. You . . . you ever get scared?"

Moony remembered seeing Notch's grandfather at the Center Tree on the night he met Magi. He wondered what the old man was doing there, staring out at the Forbidden

Watchtower.

"I do get scared sometimes," Moony said, thinking back to Burd's warning. "But I don't think we're alone in all this."

Notch squinted at him.

"What do you mean? Like you think something is watching over us? *Protecting* us?" Notch asked.

"Could be. You and I are still here, aren't we?" Moony said.

Notch shrugged.

"I've got to go. I'm trying to find my Pappy so I can show him this coin an Outskirter gave me this morning. Never seen anything like it."

Notch showed the coin to Moony.

"Hey, a man gave me one of those this morning too! But I sold it to an Outskirter," Moony explained.

"Shouldn't have sold it until you knew how much it's worth. Outskirters are always swindling Hobblers. Like Old Man Wren back before the Old War. I read about him just last month. The coin could be worth as much as a dozen tokens, for all we know!" Notch said as he rode around the corner on his bike. "See ya', Moony!"

Moony smiled, deciding he had made a pretty good deal by his one hundred tokens, then he continued on his way.

As always, the porch of Nubb Plotterdub's Weapons Shop was dark and quiet. The trading post was often visited by hunters and trappers, but most Hobblers steered away from it, a place where dark deals were made and dangerous secrets exchanged. But Burd's prophecy weighed heavy on Moony's mind. He knew a time would come when he would need to protect himself.

Moony opened the screen door, and walked into the quiet room, his bag of tokens jingling with each step.

Inside the shop were shelves of relics and glass cases filled with weapons gathered from the ancient battlegrounds of the Lostwood, passed down through generations of Hobblers. The dim room was ornamented with knives and throwing stars, crossbows and iron arrows, darts and blowguns.

Nubb sat in a wooden chair with his boots propped up on the countertop, smoking a thick cigar. Moony had not seen him since the secret barn meeting. The rugged man stared at Moony in silence and blew a smoke ring the size of a pumpkin.

Could he somehow know I overheard the secret conversation in the barn? Moony wondered.

The stable boy nodded a silent greeting and walked around the room, peering in glass cases and examining exotic items chained to the shelves.

"What'll it be, lad? A boomerang crossbow? A stick of dynamite?" Nubb asked.

Moony approached a glass case filled with rusted relics from the Old War.

"I was looking for something a little easier to handle," Moony explained, speaking toward the glass case, rather than to Nubb.

"That case is full of worthy companions," Nubb assured, walking over to Moony. "But a boy your size may need something from another case—"

But Moony quickly resolved, "I already found what I'm looking for."

A look of curiosity grew across Nubb's face, and he looked down in surprise at Moony's weapon of choice.

The shopkeeper shook his head in astonishment.

"It's quite strange that you would choose this particular saber, lad," Nubb said, scratching his beard.

"Why?" Moony asked.

Nubb unlocked the case and lifted out the sword, no bigger than a machete. He unsheathed the silver blade and held it into the lanternlight.

The gruff man then revealed, "Because this saber once belonged to your grandmother, Gem. Sold it to me twelve years ago, on the day you were born."

Chapter 19:

Shadows And Glass

When Moony saw his grandmother that evening, he made no mention of the silver saber. The old woman sat on her stool next to the fireplace, carefully crafting a new glass figurine.

Ever since the secret barn meeting, Gem had seemed like a stranger to Moony. He was beginning to realize that everyone in Hobble had secrets.

Gem finished the glass figurine and stood to place it on the fireplace mantel.

Moony suddenly recognized its shape.

"A broomstick," he whispered.

Right then, Beatrice walked into the Fireside Room, looking anxious and troubled.

"Hallows Eve is but a week away, and the jack o' lanterns from last month are all rotten. Stinkin' up the porch, they are. Moony, why don't you take the wheelbarrow over to the pumpkin farm? Go on, and bring us back half a dozen ripe ones. We can't afford to have them delivered here. I just ran into Scooter and Stokely Scabbins, and they said Gabbo would give us a deal. Said he's desperate to get rid of this month's harvest."

Jezzy, who was washing dirty dishes in the washing tub, peeked over the counter and piped in, "Oh can I go too?! It sounds like a job for both of us!"

Beatrice placed her hands on her hips and interrogated, "How you feelin', Jezzy? Still tired?"

Beatrice walked across the room and felt Jezzy's head. The fever had run its course.

"Just having a few nightmares, that's all. Other than that, I feel fine," Jezzy assured. "The medicine Moony bought me worked like a charm."

"Well, your big brother's a hero, ain't he?" Beatrice said with a smile. "Saved your life, and saved the Candletin, all in the same October. C.C. Pottleman would be knockin' down our door, threatening to kick us out on the streets if it weren't for Moony givin' us enough tokens for the rent. Our family is in good hands with a man like Moony lookin' after us. Wouldn't you say, ladies?"

Gem and Jezzy cheered in agreement.

Moony turned as red as an apple.

"Speaking of those tokens, Moony. I figured you'd have bought yourself a glyder from the Flytemasters by now. You've wanted one since you were a tot," Beatrice prodded.

Moony shifted uncomfortably in his seat. "I—I don't really need one anymore. Besides, there's better things to spend my tokens on."

Beatrice squinted her eyes, surprised by her son's lack of interest in the one thing he had always desired.

She shook her head, and continued, "I mean it, boy, you deserve it. You're a hero to this family. Your Pa and Grandpa would be proud of the man you're becoming."

Moony glowed inside at his mother's words.

Beatrice turned to Jezzy and observed the little girl to make sure she was not fibbing about feeling better.

"I suppose it's alright for you to go along with Moony, so long as you keep your fingers and toes covered. But be careful. *Lots* of kids missing in town. Scares me so. Just this morning I heard Tubb Wiggins vanished like the rest of 'em, just like the mayor hisself."

Gabbo Scabbins filled the Jarman's wheelbarrow with half a dozen bright orange pumpkins. Moony paid Gabbo half a token for each, then pushed the wheelbarrow back toward the inn, while Jezzy skipped happily alongside him.

When they reached Midnight Creek, she stopped in the middle of the bridge, and asked softly, "Do you think Joseph will ever come back?"

Moony peered down at the mound of pumpkins, not wanting to look into Jezzy's eyes.

"Why do you call him 'Joseph', Jezzy?" Moony asked. "He's our father."

"But I never knew him. And everyone says he was a bad man, and that he was the one who killed Jayden," Jezzy replied.

"Yeah, I know. But just because everyone says something doesn't mean it's true," Moony said, softly.

"He's our father. You shouldn't talk poorly of family, no matter what they've done."

There was a long period of silence before either said another word. They had not spoken of their father in many Octobers, and often wondered if he was dead. Jezzy had never known him. He had disappeared when she was just a baby, and Moony could hardly recall his face.

"Then why do you and Mom talk so badly about C.C. Pottleman?" Jezzy asked. "After all, he's Mom's father—*our* grandfather."

"Pottleman's different," Moony said. "It's okay not to like him."

"But if we liked him, maybe he'd be nicer to us. Maybe he'd give us some of his tokens. Isn't that what grandfathers do?" Jezzy proposed.

"We don't need his tokens. We fend just fine on our own," Moony replied.

Suddenly, Jezzy pointed up to the sky and shouted, "Did you see that, Moony?! Did you see it?!"

"See what?" Moony asked, following the direction of her finger.

"Those shapes flying into the clouds," Jezzy said in wonder. "They looked like—like people."

"You're just seeing things," Moony assured.

But he knew the shapes were not illusions. He had seen them too.

Chapter 20:

The Power Of The Light

A few nights later, Moony lay in the barn loft trying to get a handle on how everything he had seen and experienced during the previous month might be connected.

It was as complex as a spider's web.

Moony placed his hand over his chest, thinking of the Luminary which lay buried deep beneath his flesh. Next, he grazed his fingers over the wing tattoo just below the back of his neck. The tattoo had raised his skin, and it was still tender to touch.

All week Moony had practiced his flight in secret. If anyone saw him fly, the ancient secret of the Protectors could be discovered. Moony knew the burden was his, and his alone, to bear.

He listened to the Clock Tower strike three times in the distance.

The witching hour, he thought.

Moony sat up in his bed and retrieved his new saber from the hay bale. The sword lay hidden alongside the Moonblood compass, the moonlight letter, and his bag of tokens now considerably lighter after C.C. Pottleman had dug his greedy fingers into it. Moony strapped the blade to his back, picked up his lantern, and soared upward through the open skylight of the barn, brushing past the moon chimes as he ascended into the night sky above.

The stable boy flew over the sleeping cottages and twinkling shops of Hobble, whisked past the town's southern wall, and tumbled hard into the graveyard. He still had not mastered his landings.

Moony dusted himself off, and called out into the darkness, "Magi? Are you there? Can you hear me?"

Suddenly, a spiraling fog poured into the hazy moonlight and formed into the shape of the ghost.

"I see you've chosen your first power. Ah, and you found yourself a weapon," Magi said in his owl-like voice, admiring Moony's silver saber.

"I was hoping you'd be here," Moony said. " I have so many questions."

"As you should. But know that I am here only to encourage your questions, not to answer them," the old ghost replied.

Moony nodded, discouraged. He had hoped Magi would be more helpful, and offer him some answers.

"Tell me why you have come tonight, Moony."

"I think I know who's taking all the kids in Hobble," Moony revealed.

Magi smiled. "Then why haven't you saved them, my boy?"

The Protector looked down at the ground.

"Because it's hard to trust my suspicions. And I don't know *how* to save the kids," he confessed.

Magi said nothing, but waited for Moony to continue.

Moony's feet rose a few inches off the ground, a nervous habit he had recently acquired. "It's just—I'm—I'm just a stable boy. I've never done anything like this, and it's hard when I can't talk to anyone about it. I can't ask my family for help. And you're—well, you're dead. I'm all alone in this."

Magi wrapped his foggy arm over Moony's shoulder, and the two hovered slowly over the sea of graves.

"In many ways, you *are* alone," Magi began. "But in other ways, you are not. There are many forces of Light at work in Hobble, even among your peers. There is hope yet. You must trust that the Light is greater than the Darkness."

"I will. But what am I supposed to *do*? What if my suspicions are wrong?" Moony asked.

"You must trust your heart and your instincts. You will know what to do when the time comes. And remember, you are not only the Protector of Hobble, but also the Protector of the Moonblood secret."

Moony nodded.

Magi faced Moony as they hovered above the mausoleum where Pappy Cricklewood had been interred earlier that morning.

"You must always be true to what you are, Moony. The Luminary is within you, therefore you are a powerful vessel for the Light. All souls have the choice, and you have chosen to be guided by the power of the Light."

"But what does that mean?" Moony asked.

Magi seemed to glow brighter as he answered, "It means you have dared to hand yourself over to something far larger than yourself and have surrendered your life to a greater power. A time of darkness is upon us, Moony, and you are the only way Hobble will survive. The time for doubts has long passed. You must be ready. The Vothlor is coming, and the Black Candle will soon be lit."

"But what will happen when the Candle is lit?" Moony questioned.

Magi closed his eyes and whispered, "The new war begins."

Chapter 21:

Sleepwalker

Two days before Hallows Eve, Principal Crisp ordered that the Hobble School Of Nonsensicals be closed down until the mystery of the recent vanishings was solved.

The dozen remaining students climbed onto their burlap sacks, and slid down the tin super slides, which spiraled from the third floor windows of the schoolhouse into the landing pad of hay bales below. But the boys did not strike up games of jacks and marbles in the street as usual, nor did the girls cartwheel across the East Bridge to sing and jump rope in the festival field. Instead, all the disheartened children hung their heads, and returned to their homes as their parents had instructed them to do.

Jezzy Jarman whisked down the super slide and landed in the mountain of hay bales, quickly followed by her three friends—Mace, Milky, and Alice Scabbins. All four children dug their books out of the hay, and climbed off the golden landing pad.

"Another dozen kids gone missing in two days. Think we're next?" Mace asked, cradling his favorite book, *How To Trap A Swamp Monster*.

"Probably. The Elders are scared for us. They say our nightmares are a bad omen," Alice said with concern. "The *Gazette* said if something happens to the last of us, there won't be any future for Hobble. After all those kids were killed during the Old War, Hobble was almost wiped out."

"Ah, ain't nothin' gonna happen to us," Mace assured. "We'd have been 'napped by now. You jus' been listenin' to Scooter and Stokely's spook stories. Besides, if anyone gets taken, it's their own fault for being stupid."

"That's a terrible thing to say," Jezzy remarked, peeking her big, brown eyes over the top of the book she clutched in her arms—*Secrets Of The Mountain Witches, Volume One*.

"Ah, I'm just kiddin', Jezzy," Mace assured. "Say, let's all go to the bakery for another taste of the brew. That'll cheer us up."

Mace, Milky, and Alice clicked their heels in the air and ran toward Town Square to visit Gubbles' Goodies.

But Jezzy stayed behind.

"Come on, Jezzy!" Alice called back to her. "Everyone's already tried it except for you!"

"Yeah, come on, Jezzy," Milky added.

Jezzy had doted on Milky Scabbins for nearly two months before she caught her fever, and she did not want him to think she was afraid.

But she remembered Moony's warning, and reluctantly replied, "No thanks. My brother said—"

"It ain't gonna hurt you. Besides, Moony don't have to

know," Mace interjected.

Jezzy thought of Moony's warning on the day he caught her waiting in line for a taste of the brew. She looked over and saw chimney smoke spiraling upward from the direction of the Candletin Inn.

"Let's go, Jezzy! Time's a wastin'! The line's probably already piled out the door," Milky encouraged.

Jezzy sighed in surrender, and ran after her friends.

Late that night, the back door of the inn creaked open, then slammed shut like thunder.

Moony awoke at the sound and quickly sat up in his bed. It was the dead of night, and all of Hobble was asleep. He looked up through the open skylight and examined the constellations. The stars seemed dimmer. Something evil was afoot, and he sensed danger.

Moony flew up through the skylight and crouched on the roof of the barn. His hair bristled in the breeze and his ears perked to the sounds of the night. He peered down at the inn, and saw Jezzy heading around the corner toward Town Square.

"Jezzy!" Moony called out to her, but she did not hear him.

Moony wanted to fly after her, but he hesitated. If any Hobbler happened to be watching from a darkened window or a porch swing, his identity could be discovered. He swiftly flew back down into the barn, and landed on his feet just before running out the barn door.

He rushed around the corner of the inn and called for Jezzy, but she was nowhere in sight.

Down the street, something moved. Something squeaked.

Moony saw the back door of Gubbles' Goodies swing shut like a coffin lid, and he quickly ran toward the bakery. His bare feet thumped against the cobblestones as he jumped over wooden barrels and swung around lampposts, running as fast as he could toward the bakery door.

He reached for the copper knob and tried to turn it with both hands . . .

but it was locked.

Moony pounded on the door and called out, "Jezzy! Jezzy! Are you in there?"

But no one answered his calls.

Jezzy was gone.

Chapter 22:

Through The Spyglass

Moony burst through the door of the upstairs apartment at the inn and woke Beatrice and Gem. Both women quickly sat up in their beds and lit the lanterns on their nightstands. A mist of golden light filled the bedroom and cast their shadows upon the walls.

"What's wrong, Moony?" Beatrice asked in concern.

"Jezzy's gone!" Moony cried out breathlessly.

"What do you mean, boy?"

"I saw her walk out the back door of the inn. Then I followed her to the bakery, and watched her go inside. But when I tried to open the door, it was locked. Hurry, we have to save her!"

"Calm down, boy. Calm down. It sounds like you had a nightmare," Gem assuaged. "It's to be expected, especially the way things are going."

"No, Grammy, I saw it with my own eyes. Jezzy's in the bakery right now!"

"Oh, she'll be alright, then," Gem assured in a calm

voice.

"Yes, I'm sure she'll be home soon," Beatrice added.

"But you don't understand! We have to go save her *now*! Before it's too late!" Moony cried out.

"Why don't we go downstairs and calm you down with a cup of cocoa? That'll ease your worries," his mother said.

Gem and Beatrice made their way to the Fireside Room, and Moony followed after them, puzzled by their lack of concern. It was as if they knew something he didn't know.

Beatrice kindled a fire in the hearth and placed a kettle of cocoa over the flames. When the chocolaty concoction was warm enough, she poured a cup and urged Moony to sit at the table and drink. She left the Fireside Room and then disappeared out the screen door of the kitchen.

Gem took a seat on her stool next to the fireplace.

A thought struck Moony. *Could my own family be working with the Vothlor?*

He shook his head, unwilling to accept it. But all the signs pointed to them hiding secrets. First, the conversations in the barn. Now, they seemed content that Jezzy was missing along with the others.

Gem smiled at her grandson.

"All will turn out right in the end, Moony. You need not worry yourself," she said.

The old woman had covered her newest glass figurine with a tattered cloth the night before, and left it on the ledge of the fireplace to cool overnight. She rubbed her hands together in excitement, and pulled the cloth away to unveil her newest creation. The glass figurine was a terrifying creature—a cloaked figure that was completely hollow.

Gem looked upon the figure in puzzlement, as if she had hoped it to be something different.

"Grammy?" Moony finally spoke.

Gem was startled at the sound of his voice.

"Yes, dear?" she asked softly.

Moony hesitated, then asked, "Have you ever owned a saber?"

Gem's eyes widened in surprise, and she shook her head.

"Not that I can rememb—"

Right then, Moony lifted his hands from beneath the table and revealed the saber to his grandmother. He had hidden the weapon beneath the table the evening before so he could ask her about its origins.

"Oh, why yes," she confessed, with flushed cheeks. "I knew that saber long ago."

Moony continued, "Nubb Plotterdub told me you sold it to him on the day I was born."

"Did he?" Gem replied, shortly.

Moony nodded, then asked, "Why'd you sell it?"

"We needed the money, and I no longer had any use for it. But I always suspected this saber might find its way back into the family." She smiled at Moony, and continued, "You might as well have the other piece."

Gem stood from her chair and counted the bricks on the left side of the fireplace—twelve up and six over. She shook the brick loose from the wall, reached her arm into the hollow, and removed a narrow wooden box.

"The saber was part of a set," Gem revealed. "They say these two pieces are magical. Forged from the strongest iron known to Hobblers and Jypsis alike. Unbreakable, under any circumstances."

She walked over to the table and placed the box in front of Moony. He lifted the lid and examined the contents within.

There, cradled in purple velvet lining, was a copper spyglass.

Gem placed her hand on Moony's shoulders and added in a soft, wistful voice, "Belonged to your Grandpa Rufus, in fact."

By the following night, Jezzy still had not returned to the inn.

Just before the witching hour, Moony snuck out of the barn and waited in the shadows behind the bakery. He hid behind an empty cider barrel, and soon noticed candlelight flickering in an upstairs window. He quietly flew to the roof, and found two circles had been rubbed into the soot of the windowpane, as if someone had recently looked inside.

He pressed his face against the glass, and saw a candle glowing from a nightstand in the corner of the room. Just below the nightstand, he saw what looked like a woman, lying on the floor.

"Plumb," Moony whispered in horror.

The beloved baker was tied to the bed posts, with a red bandana stuffed in her mouth. Her eyes were closed, and Moony did not know if she was asleep, or dead. One thing was clear—Plumb was in danger.

Suddenly, Plumb's drowsy eyes opened, and her gaze fell upon the boy at the window. She quickly sat up, and desperately called for help, but the gag muffled her words. Moony attempted to open the window, but it was locked. He wrapped the cuff of his shirt around his fist, and busted through the glass, then cautiously climbed inside the dim room, which smelled of rotten flesh.

He whispered to the frightened baker, "It's alright, Plumb. I'm gonna get you out of here."

Plumb looked up at her savior with desperate eyes.

Moony took the candle from the nightstand, and was horrified by what he saw next. All around the room, on shelves and the floor, were blood-spattered jars full of eyes, ears, teeth, noses, and strips of flesh. He wondered what horrors Plumb had witnessed during the past month, and what the Gubbles had done with his own sister.

Tears formed in Plumb's eyes as Moony untied her arms and legs and removed the gag from her mouth.

"Thank you, boy," she managed to speak through chapped lips. "I thought I would die here in this nightmare."

"Everything's going to be alright, I promise," Moony assured. "What have the Gubbles done to you?"

"Terrible things, boy. They abducted me in my sleep the night after the Star Festival, and I've been tied up here in my own room ever since. Is everyone in town alright?"

Moony looked out the broken window to the silent night, then back to the captive baker.

"Hobble's changed, Plumb. Several of the Elders have been murdered, and most of the children have gone missing. They think Malivar is coming back with the

Vothlor," Moony said, fearing for Jezzy's life. "Where are the Gubbles now?"

"Below in the kitchen. Heard them not an hour ago, cooking something in the cauldrons," Plumb said, paled by the grim news about the gatekeepers and the children.

"The brew," Moony whispered.

He put his ear to the bedroom door, and listened. He heard the voices of the Gubbles down the stairwell, chanting an eerie song.

"We have to get you out of here," Moony said. "We have to tell Sheriff what's happened."

And with that, Moony helped Plumb out the window. Before he followed her out, he glanced back at the jars of eyeballs and ears and noses and fingers, and wondered upon the use of such monstrosities.

Could that be what the Gubbles are using in their brew?

Moony helped lower Plumb from the roof to the drainage pipe. When they arrived on the ground, he noticed Plumb could barely walk.

"Can you make it to Sheriff's?" Moony asked.

"I think so," Plumb replied, rubbing her wrists. "Where are you going?"

"I have to find out what the Gubbles are up to so I can put an end to this," Moony said.

"Be careful," Plumb warned. "There's no tellin' what the Gubbles will do to you if they catch you."

Plumb kissed Moony's forehead and thanked him, then hobbled around the corner toward the jailhouse. Moony ducked behind a cider barrel outside the bakery, and waited.

As soon as the Clock Tower struck three o' clock, three shadows flew out of the chimney like puffs of black smoke. The figures ascended into the cloudy sky, and soared toward the eastern Lostwood.

Moony quickly flew after the three broomsticks.

The October air chilled his face as he soared up into the dark night. He stayed a safe distance behind the wicked trio, and watched as they descended into the Lostwood about a mile away from the Mountain Of Light.

Moony hovered down through the treetops and landed behind a bumpkin bush.

Peering over the hedge, he watched the trio approach the mouth of a cave that opened beneath a rocky cliff. An eerie glow flickered from within the cave, illuminating the sinister beauty of Vivy, Issa, and Gertrude Gubble.

Two figures guarded each side of the cave's entrance. They were half as tall as the Gubble sisters, but twice as wide, and each held an enormous spear.

Moony took out his copper spyglass to gain a more detailed view.

"Goblins," he whispered.

He crept closer, sneaking from bush to bush until he was only two-dozen feet from the entrance of the cave. The Gubble sisters approached the guards.

"Seen any spies tonight, Toadnickle?" Vivy asked the goblin on the right side of the cave.

The wild-haired creature chuckled a rugged, broken laugh.

"None yet," Toadnickle said.

"Good," Vivy replied. "Then everything is in place. Tomorrow night will be your last night to stand guard.

After midnight of Hallows Eve, the bodies will be here no more."

Moony's heart dropped into his stomach. He wanted nothing more than to fly out from behind the bushes and rescue Jezzy and the other vanished children.

But I'll never make it past those goblins without being speared and eaten, he decided, wishing he had more courage—and a plan.

Then, in the torchlight twinkling at the mouth of the cave, Moony saw something so horrifying he did not believe it to be real.

There, behind the two goblins, a thousand black, empty sockets stared back at Moony.

From the skulls of murdered children.

Chapter 23:

A Voice In The Wind

All Hallows Eve arrived like a dusty dream . . .

Moony did not speak to anyone of what he had seen the night before, feeling sickened by the sight of the children's skulls. He trusted that Plumb had given a detailed report to Sheriff, and a plot was already underway to arrest the Gubbles. But still, Moony's heart was unsettled. He knew that normal Hobblers were no match for the powers of the Gubble sisters, and that only he could rescue whatever children remained alive. He hoped with all his heart that Jezzy was among them.

After Moony finished his chores, he fetched his bag of tokens from the barn loft, and went to visit the apothecary. A single jack o' lantern sat at the front of the shop, and a dozen black cats perched upon tabletops and ceiling rafters, staring back at Moony with lazy yellow eyes.

Burd Trubbles sat behind the front counter with her

eyes shut.

Is she asleep? Moony wondered.

The old frump sniffed the air with her long, crooked nose and said, "Ah, young Jarman. Didn't think you'd be back so soon."

"How'd you know it was me?" he asked.

Burd smiled her toothless grin and replied, "Hay and cider. It's been your scent ever since you was a tot. I could smell you from outside the door. Smell like your father used to smell. Your granddaddy too. Now, what can I do for you, lad? Is your little sister back to health?"

Moony looked down at the ground at the mention of Jezzy.

"Ah, so she's gone missin' with the others," the old woman surmised.

Moony softly replied, "Yes."

"Ain't surprised. I smelled her outside the bakery a few days ago. There's something in that brew if you ask me— something strange."

Moony wondered if Burd knew even more than what she had revealed.

"What do *you* think's in it?" he asked, hoping it was not the jarred body parts he had seen in the upstairs bedroom.

But Burd had begun busily dusting the shelves with her feather-sweep. Moony walked over to a nearby shelf, where he reached for a long, flute-like contraption with a small funnel attached to its end.

"I'd like to buy this blowgun and a dozen sleep darts," he requested.

"Ain't for sale. Bought it from Nubb Plotterdub not two weeks ago. What might you need such a weapon for,

---

103

anyways?" Burd asked.

"Hunting," Moony lied. "I'm going on a boar hunt, and I need a blowgun and a dozen sleep darts. The butcher pays high dollar for live boar."

The apothecary smiled.

"Strange that a boy who had a sack full of tokens only a few days ago is already in need of some more, and willing to risk his life by hunting wild boar in the Lostwood at a time like this," Burd pried. "Alright then, I'll sell the blowgun to you—market price."

She walked over to a shelf holding dozens of jars, all filled with colored powders and gooey liquids. Burd sniffed her way along the row of jars and lifted the lid off one which read, *Agrimony and Clary Sage*.

"How strong do you need the sleep potion to be for your—" Burd paused, then continued, "for your 'boar hunt'?"

Moony cleared his throat and replied, "Strong enough to put, say, a *goblin* to sleep."

Burd nodded, knowingly. She picked up a feathered dart and dipped the needlepoint into the black liquid inside the open jar. Altogether, she sunk a dozen darts into the oily slime, waited for the sleeping potion to harden on the end of the needles, then wrapped the whole lot in a black leather pouch and handed it to Moony.

Moony placed the pouch in his trouser pocket and paid Burd.

As he turned to walk out the door of the shop, the old woman called after him.

"The neck," she said. "It's the best place to attack a—" she paused and smiled. "—a boar."

That evening, the sunset sky was an eerie green. A parade of black clouds converged over the southern Lostwood, and a northerly wind blew cold and strong.

A storm was coming. It would hit Hobble no later than midnight.

Moony soared through the air above the river and landed atop the Protector's Sanctuary.

Inside, Gimble stood on a chair in the kitchen, stirring a boiling pot of stew.

"Pizzlebugs?" Gimble called over his shoulder.

He jumped down from his perch and offered a plate of slimy blue bugs to Moony.

"No, no thank you," Moony replied.

"Thought you might be comin' around tonight. Hallows Eve is always a busy night for the Protector," Gimble said, casually. "So what's the conundrum this October?"

Moony hesitated to speak, but then remembered Gimble had heard many secrets through the centuries . . . and seen many Protectors die.

"I found all the missing children of Hobble in a goblin cave last night. And I know who put them there."

"The children are in a cave, you say?" Gimble replied, as if it were somehow familiar to him. "I've heard this story before. Was a very long time ago though. If I remember it right, they all died."

"How?" Moony questioned.

"Don't know exactly," Gimble replied. "But I believe those who refused the mark of the ⚡ were destroyed, and

---

105

those who took the mark were spared. Terrible tragedy."

"Was it three witch sisters who did the murders?" Moony persisted.

"Couldn't say." The little man paused and observed Moony from head to toe. "We had better get you geared up for the night."

Gimble led Moony through the Hallway Of Stories, where the former Protectors stared at the newest Protector from within their stained glass windows. Gimble opened up a wardrobe at the end of the gallery and rifled through the various weapons and pieces of armor. After a few moments, he removed a leather cross belt from the bottom drawer and held it up to Moony.

"This should do," the little man said. "It belonged to a great Protector long ago."

Gimble strapped the double cross belt over Moony's shoulders and around his hips. A small diamond flickered on the cross straps over his chest. The little man then fastened the copper spyglass, the bronze compass, the black blowgun, and the sleeping darts to the leather straps. Lastly, he slid the silver saber into a sheath on Moony's back, then stepped back to double-check his handiwork.

"Never seen a Protector so fierce in all my years," Gimble affirmed.

Moony smiled and shook Gimble's hand.

"Thank you, Gimble," Moony said, and placed his other hand on Gimble's shoulder.

The little man blushed bashfully, and grunted, "Don't mention it, boy. You best be off on your adventure. Storm's a comin'."

Moony smiled, climbed up to the crow's nest of the

sanctuary, and flew away into the darkening night, rocketing toward Hobble.

As the little man watched the stable boy fly away, he whispered, "Be careful, boy. Those empowered by Malivar possess powers far greater than any Protector can imagine."

High up in the sky, Moony looked back over his shoulder and saw the storm drawing near. Lightning danced across the vast blackness, and the wind howled around him like a pack of hungry wolves.

A few moments later, he landed on the roof of Gubbles' Goodies. He wanted to make sure the few remaining children in town were not being lulled into the sisters' trap. But no smoke swirled out of the bakery's chimney, and he heard no voices within the darkened shop.

But just before Moony launched from the roof to go to the cave, he heard a voice cry out for help nearby. He glanced down at the street below and saw the dark, raven hair of a girl dressed in overalls running out of the bakery.

The girl was screaming in panic.

Moony flew down behind her, and she turned around just as his feet touched the ground.

A look of horror plagued her eyes, and she cried out to Moony, "They took him! The Gubbles took my brother!"

Moony put out his hand to calm the girl whom he knew from the pumpkin farm.

It was Stokely Scabbins.

Right then, the Clock Tower struck eleven 'o clock—one hour until midnight.

Chapter 24:

Cave Of Skulls

"I know where they're taking your brother," Moony told Stokely.

The wind whirled around them as they stood in front of the bakery and listened to the Clock Tower strike its eleventh gong. A sharp flash of purple light lit up the Lostwood beyond the southern wall, where Notch Cricklewood had ridden his bike a few moments before.

"Tell me where!" Stokely demanded. "We have to save him! It's all my fault. I never should have left him."

"They took him to a goblin cave a mile west of the Light Mines. All the kids are there," he revealed, not wanting to frighten her with the whole truth of it. "We still have time to save them—I think. At least some of them."

Stokely stared at Moony, puzzled by his claim. She noted the weaponry on his leather cross belt—the golden spyglass, the bronze compass, the black blowgun, the dozen sleep darts, and the silver saber. He looked like he was dressed to go trick-or-treating.

"Here, take this," Moony pressed the compass into Stokely's hand.

"What is it?" she asked.

"A compass. It'll lead you to the cave," Moony explained. "Follow the hunting paths northeast. The compass will take you to the right place. Just trust the coordinates. Hide in the bushes outside the cave 'til I get there."

"Wait, where are you going?" Stokely questioned.

"I have to take care of something first," Moony explained. "It won't take long. But you should go on ahead. Now."

Moony then noticed something hidden in the shadows of the street. He held up his lantern, and there, parked near the Light Dock, was an electro-wagon made of. . . junkyard parts?

A single word was painted onto its side: *Starwagon*.

Moony turned to Stokely and instructed, "Try driving that thing to the cave. It should get you there faster."

Stokely ran to the Starwagon and jumped into the driver's seat. She slammed her foot down on the pedalboard, and felt the wheels churning over the cobblestones. Moony watched her zoom past the Fiddler's well and through the Crescent Gates, where Deputy Notwod was far too slow getting up from his stool to stop her.

When Moony was sure the Starwagon was out of sight, he soared up into the stormy sky with his lantern held out before him like a rising star. After several miles of flight above the clouds, he descended into the Lostwood, and hid in the bushes outside the cave.

The two goblins, Toadnickle and Wartooth, stood outside the cave, sipping a dark liquid from one of the skulls. The air smelled of blood, and Moony feared the executions had already begun. Knowing there was no time to waste, he dropped a dart into the blowgun's chamber and carefully aimed at Wartooth's rubbery, wart-covered neck, just as Burd had instructed.

Moony blew with all his might.

When the dart penetrated the goblin's thick flesh, Wartooth dropped his skull of goblin brew and grabbed at his wound, but it was too late.

Toadnickle observed his fallen companion and brandished his spear toward the darkness. But just as he caught sight of Moony in the bushes, a dart entered the goblin's knobby flesh, and he fell right on top of Wartooth.

Moony couldn't help but smile at his first success as Protector.

Suddenly, the trees of the forest shook like a derailed train. A violent wind whistled through the air, but the faint torchlight at the mouth of the cave remained still and bright.

The storm had arrived.

Moony slipped past the goblins, and moved toward the pile of skulls just inside the mouth of the cave.

Jezzy's skull could be among this massive pile, he feared.

He stepped deeper into the chamber, and carefully removed a torch from the rock wall. Moony held the light out before him, but saw no sign of the children.

Slowly, he raised the torch above his head.

He squinted his eyes, and soon noticed that strange pockets had been carved out of the cave walls. Tucked into the cubbies, were dozens of strange statues glimmering in the torchlight.

Moony flew up to the wall. Hovering in mid-air, he reached out and touched one of the statues. His eyes filled with horror, and his heart pounded in his chest. For these were not statues at all, but children . . .

made of wax.

Red Crisp stared back at him with glazed eyes, and Moony wondered if the paperboy could still be alive inside his wax shell. He tried to rouse Red, but the boy remained still and cold—frozen in some horrible spell, sitting atop his waxed bike with a Gazette satchel over his shoulder. He seemed unreal, like a bizarre doll.

When Moony flew to the next statue, the pale face of a young boy looked back at him with wide, foggy eyes—as if he had turned into wax in the middle of being scared by something. The waxed boy held a boxlite in his frosted hand. It was Hoot Cricklewood, who had disappeared with the eleven other kids while playing Goblinlight. Moony scanned the remaining rows of statues extending far into the back of the cave. It looked like a collection of toys.

He detached Hoot's wax statue from its slot in the wall, and flew with it out of the cave and to a safe place, a place he knew the Gubbles would never think to look. Then he returned to the cave, and, one by one, flew all of the spellbound children to safety. Finally, he found Jezzy.

After placing his sister in the secret hideaway, Moony returned to the cave and found the Starwagon parked behind the bushes. But when he searched the bushes for Stokely, he found only her red bandana lying on the ground.

Chapter 25:

As Good As Dead

The Hallows Eve wind howled through the trees as a swarm of bats poured out of the cave and scattered into the green-tinted night. Lightning flickered in the swirling clouds above, and a few raindrops began to sprinkle the ground.

Moony searched for any other sign of Stokely.

"Hey! Over here!" a loud whisper threaded through the wind.

Moony looked beyond the swaying bushes and saw Stokely crouched behind the Starwagon. He ran to her, and she quickly snatched her bandana from his hand.

"Thanks, it must have fallen out of my overalls," she said. "Say, how'd you get here so fast?"

Right then, Moony heard a sharp creaking sound at the edge of the forest. He and Stokely turned to see three slithering figures climb out of a secret door built into the forest floor between two towering trees. The Gubble sisters dragged both a limp Scooter Scabbins and a large sack toward the cave.

"We must get these boys waxed before midnight," one of the sisters said. "Malivar will be in Hobble soon, and the marking ceremony will begin."

"The Gubbles!" Stokely whispered in rage. "What should we do?"

"You stay here," Moony commanded. "And out of sight."

"But I'm supposed to save him!" Stokely called, but Moony was already beyond earshot.

He snuck around the Starwagon, and followed after the Gubbles.

At the sight of the fallen goblin guards, the sisters rushed into the empty cave. They began screaming, and their shrill cries echoed off the stone walls and down the dark throat of the cavern.

Moony walked out of the shadows and calmly called out to the Gubbles, "From the first time I stepped into the bakery, I knew there was something evil in your brew."

The Gubble sisters spun around at the sound of Moony's voice.

"Where are they?! Where are the children?!" Issa shrieked.

Moony stepped further into the cave.

"Someplace you'll never find them. Now, hand over Scooter and whoever is in that sack. This all ends here."

Vivy Gubble stepped towards Moony.

"You fool!" she yelled. "We brought the children here to *save* them, by Mayor Waddletub's orders! Malivar has risen, and this cave was the best chance the children had of surviving. Now, they're all as good as dead!"

Chapter 26:

Moment Of Truth

Right then, a rickety sound echoed out of the forest. A soft glow swelled in the deep darkness, until a black stagecoach appeared—with a purple lantern gleaming at its prow.

The man in the dusty top hat sat atop the driver's perch, whipping the wagon's four black stallions. This was the same man who had given Moony the Topkins coin back in the Candletin a few days before. Moony also noticed that in the place of the fifth horse was a stranger whose face was covered with a burlap sack and whose deformed hands were tied together behind his back. Moony thought it looked like the man he had seen run out of the museum on the night he had lifted the meteorite from the crater in Town Square.

"He's here!" Gertrude whispered. "Malivar has found

us! Save yourself, boy!"

Issa dragged Scooter's unconscious body behind a boulder, while Vivy and Gertrude together lifted the black bag and scurried after her.

Vivy called out to Moony, who stood still as a statue, "Hide yourself, boy! Hide before he enters! He'll grant you no mercy!"

Moony broke free from his trance, and hid behind the pile of yellow skulls.

Outside the cave, the man in the top hat whipped the captive wearing the burlap mask again and again, and Moony could hear the prisoner whimper at each strike. But the mouth of the prisoner sounded muffled, as if he were gagged. Moony peered through the pile of skulls, and saw tears in the eyes of the man behind the mask.

"That'll teach you to stay away from our meetings and out of our business, *Son*," the man in the top hat shouted, then whipped the prisoner once again. "To think you've been alive all this time! Living as a monster! I know just what to do with you! You're a freak, and you'll go where freaks belong!"

Suddenly, all fell into complete silence.

The door of the stagecoach opened up, and Moony realized there was someone inside the cab of the wagon.

A skinny silhouette crept out of the wagon, and turned toward the purple lanternlight. It was Tobo Jingles. He carried himself with a new confidence, as if some power had infected him. The Toymaster held open the door, and waited, as if there was yet another passenger in the night wagon.

Moony felt his breath quickening. Finally, an ominous,

cloaked figure slowly stepped out of the stagecoach without saying a word. Tobo bowed his head, as if humbling himself.

Moony watched as a shrouded creature approached the cave of skulls, dragging its leg with each step. The phantom stopped, sniffed the air deeply, and looked directly at Moony's hiding place.

It's—it's Malivar, Moony thought, feeling a chill of terror run up his spine.

The creature purred at the sight of Moony's shadow on the wall.

"Did you like my presents, boy?" the figure spoke, its face hidden by the shadows of the hood. The familiar voice continued, "On the night of the Star Festival. In the baskets. Did you like the heads?"

Moony's heart pounded, and his eyes stung with truth and horror as he remembered the bloody heads of the gatekeepers.

Happy and Guffy's murderer is right here, he thought.

The fiend stepped into the torchlight, and removed its hood.

There, before him, was not the cloaked vapor he had expected to see. It was not Malivar, but someone Moony had known all his life—someone he had always trusted. It wasn't Gem or Nubb. Nor was it Burd Trubbles or Lilla Humplestock.

It was . . .

"Plumb!?" Moony yelled in surprise.

The baker cackled with dark, twisted laughter.

She turned to Tobo, and said, "Now, be a good boy and go fetch the circus! Take the freak along with you." She nodded at the man in the burlap mask, and his eyes glared back at her, vengefully.

"As you wish," Tobo said, then climbed up onto the driver's perch with the tall man in the top hat—the man named Silas.

Silas whipped the horses and the prisoner, and they began to gallop off into the forest. Suddenly, the stagecoach lifted up off the ground and flew up into the night. Moony watched in awe, as the stagecoach disappeared into the storm.

"It was you?!" Vivy Gubble shouted at Plumb as she and her two sisters stepped out from behind the nearby boulder. "But how?! It's impossible! All along *you* were the secret vessel, right beneath our noses—"

Plumb smiled, and her rosy cheeks beamed with dark pleasure.

"I have waited for this hour for many years—fifty to be exact," Plumb revealed.

Her voice sounded like it was *two* voices—hers and a more terrible creature living inside her.

"You will not find a another child in this cave," Issa assured. "Winky knew that when the gatekeepers were murdered and the mark of the Vothlor appeared, Malivar had somehow found a way to return. Winky feared the vanishings would take place once again, just as they did in the Old War, when Malivar killed the others through the hands of Fink Karbunkle," Issa nodded toward the pile of yellow skulls.

Plumb hissed in response.

"I was here, you know, with the others," Plumb said. "Malivar's nightmares led me to this cave when I was just a

———
119

girl. The whispers promised me the nightmares would end if I came here. And so for many months I sat in the darkness of this cave and watched the slaughter of all the children who refused to receive the mark. I was the last one, and on the night when the Black Candle was sealed, just before Malivar disappeared, he made a promise to me. He told me I would not have to die like the others if I would receive his mark and allow him to live inside of me. He promised me power, immortality, and that I would rule the Vothlor when he returned. So for fifty years, I've lived amongst you disgusting Hobblers, but all the while Malivar's voice has been with me—whispering in my thoughts. Soon, all of Hobble will belong to the Vothlor. And those who do not receive the mark will be destroyed."

The Gubbles trembled.

Gertrude narrowed her eyes and addressed the creature within Plumb, "Such trickery may have saved you fifty years ago, Malivar, but it will not save you this night. You will have to kill each one of us before you ever steal another child from Hobble's future."

"So be it," Plumb hissed. The baker flew upside-down through the air, until she came face-to-face with Vivy. "Perhaps I shall start with that saucy tongue of yours."

Moony watched as green saliva dripped out of Plumb's mouth and covered Vivy's cheek. Against her will, Vivy's tongue slowly extended past her trembling lips, and Plumb waved her hand in a slicing motion. Blood squirted onto the ground as Vivy's tongue severed, and she screamed out in pain.

The Gubbles ran to help their sister, but Plumb raised her hands, and skeins of purple light spilled out of her fingertips, strangling their necks. They gasped and writhed in agony, but could not move.

"His power fills me!" Plumb said with excitement, turning to see Scooter Scabbins lying unconscious on the floor.

Plumb hovered above Scooter's unconscious body, and ten black fingernails extended out of her fingertips and dug into Scooter's shoulders. As she opened her mouth, razor-sharp teeth approached Scooter's chest.

Next, a green slime dripped out of Plumb's mouth and covered Scooter's face as Moony reached for his saber.

But before he could attack, Stokely ran into the cold, dark cave and shouted, "Take me! Let my brother go! I'll take the mark of the **V**, just let him go free!"

Chapter 27:

Revelations

Plumb's bright, blue eyes turned grey and cold at the sight of the girl. She abandoned Scooter, and hovered through the air toward Stokely.

Stokely stood at the mouth of the cave, clenched her fists in determination, and stepped toward Plumb. She *would* heed the destiny revealed to her by the Tree Of Memories weeks before: *You must die for your brother.*

Plumb raised her clawed hands. Streams of light poured out of her black fingertips and circled Stokely's body, like a coiling snake.

Immediately, Moony soared out from behind the mound of skulls and wrapped Stokely in his arms, pulling her away from the violent current of energy. Then, in a split second, Moony flew to the boulder and scooped Scooter's unconscious body into his other arm. Before Plumb could react, Moony zipped over her balding head and out of the cave, carrying a Scabbins twin in each of his arms.

Plumb squealed in rage and disbelief as Moony soared into the stormy night.

Moony quickly glanced back at the cave to make sure he was not being followed. On his right side, lightning struck a swaying pine tree and set it on fire. Another tree, and another tree caught aflame nearby, and Moony realized it was not lightning from the sky, but fiery bolts sent out from the power of Malivar.

Moony soared as high as he could above the treeline of the Lostwood, carrying the twins back toward Hobble as the bolts zapped and sizzled all around him.

"A flying boy . . ." Plumb purred at the mouth of the cave, watching Moony carry the Scabbins twins deep into the black, trembling night.

And so Plumb lifted her cloak, ascended from the ground, and flew into the blustery night, following the scent of hay and cider on the wind.

Chapter 28:

Like A Puppet On A String

Moony hovered down from the flickering clouds, and landed next to the Tree Of The Dead.

He had dropped Scooter and Stokely in a place where he hoped Plumb would never find them. Moony knew this was his battle to fight, perhaps the very reason he had been chosen as Protector.

"Magi! Moonbloods! I need your help! Where are you?!" Moony's voice trembled as he waited for the misty spirits to pour out of the ancient trunk.

Right then, a cold drop of rain splattered upon his arm, then another on his forehead, and another on his boot. A crooked tongue of fire licked the sky, tearing open the black clouds and commanding an army of rain to pound upon the world of the Dead below.

Moony shouted at the Tree Of The Dead, "Please,

Magi! Help me! Malivar is coming!"

Just then, Plumb descended out of the swirling clouds like a giant, wicked bird. Her black, flapping cloak whipped in the wind, and another bolt of silver lightning split the sky. Moony cringed at the rotted, grey face of Plumb. She already looked twice as ugly as she had in the cave.

"Malivar is growing stronger in me every moment since the Black Candle has been lit."

Moony desperately searched the graveyard, but the storm clouds had shrouded the moon from spilling its light.

Knowing Malivar's powers were far greater than his own, Moony aimed his fists up toward the sky and lifted off into the stormy night.

"You can't escape from me, stupid boy!" Plumb laughed.

She shot streams of sizzling purple light, which pulled Moony back down to the ground like a puppet on a string. Plumb then lifted Moony and whipped him through the howling air like a kyte, slamming him into tree trunks and against crumbling tombstones.

Suddenly, Plumb's chain of purple light retracted back into her fingertips, and Moony landed face down on the muddy ground. Drops of blood rolled out of his nose and dripped onto the grass.

Have to get out of here . . . Can't last much longer.

Chapter 29:

Into The Grave

Moony rubbed his head, attempting to clear his painful daze. He pushed himself up, and ran toward the nearby woods. Just ahead of him, an iron fence with pointed spires and fanged gargoyles separated the cemetery from the Lostwood.

"Not so fast, boy!" Plumb hissed.

The web of purple light from her fingertips spread across the tombstone-covered ground. Bony hands shot up through the muddy soil like a garden of death. Moony wrenched to a stop as skeletal fingers latched onto his boot.

"All things dead and dark are subject to Malivar's will. Even the bones beneath our feet," Malivar's voice intoned through Plumb's mouth.

Skeleton hands clawed their way out of their coffins and graves, resurrected by the dark light which spilled out of Plumb's fingertips.

Moony's heart lurched with fear. Everywhere he turned another skeleton stood in his path, creeping toward him. And all the bones were solid black.

"The black skeletons all received the mark of the Vothlor during their lifetimes, and remain extensions of Malivar's will," the dark Voice threatened. "They'll hunt you down, and feast upon your delicious flesh *for me*. And *your* powers will be mine."

Moony pulled his saber from his shoulder sheath and held it out as a warning.

That's why the man who gave me the Topkins coin in the Candletin had black teeth, Moony thought. *He had the mark.*

Right then, one of the black skeletons latched onto his back, and sunk its cracked teeth into his neck. Moony spun around and slashed his blade through the skeleton's skull. The bony creature collapsed to the ground, but stood up once more, with Moony's blood dripping from its jaws.

Moony reached up and felt the bite-mark on his neck. It stung to his touch.

"Fool! You cannot kill what is already dead," Plumb shrieked. "Hundreds of corpses in this graveyard obey Malivar's command, and he commands them through me!"

When another dark skeleton slid off the tree branch above Moony's head, he quickly brandished his saber, and the skeleton shattered into a thousand tiny pieces. Next, a larger skeleton leapt toward Moony from the roof of a nearby mausoleum, and Moony jabbed his sword in between its ribs, cracking apart its bony torso. The skeleton wrapped its hands around Moony's face and tried to scrape away the boy's flesh with its chiseled fingernails. But

Moony shoved the skeleton off, withdrew his sword, and turned to run, only to see a wall of black bones in every direction. Closing in on him. While Plumb watched in malicious amusement.

"Your powers are strong, but not strong enough to save Hobble. Have no doubt, I'll find the children, and Malivar will make them choose—the mark of the 𝕐, or death. But you can make things much easier for yourself if you'll simply tell me where they are."

The skeleton army formed an inescapable circle, ready to pounce.

Death is a terrible darkness, Moony thought, as he stared into countless hollow sockets.

"*Indeed it is*," a dark voice whispered inside Moony's thoughts—Malivar's voice. A vision entered Moony's mind, and he saw himself lying cold in a grave—forever separated from the living. "*Join me now, let me live inside you, and you will never have to know what it is to end. I'll make you more powerful than you can possibly imagine.*"

"I'll never join you!" Moony cried out.

All at once, the army of skeletons charged toward Moony and attacked him with their razor-sharp fangs. He fought them as best as he could, but suddenly, a horrendous pain struck Moony's ankle. He cried out in anguish and looked down to see the sharp teeth of a skeleton piercing his flesh. Moony yelped in pain and fell to the ground. With this, the entire army of the Dead swarmed him, chanting a terrible noise as they prepared to rip away his flesh and eat his heart.

This is the way it ends, he realized.

128

But, astonishingly, Plumb waved her hands over the ground and commanded the entire army to return back to their graves. The skeletons slowly backed away, still hissing and drooling for Moony's flesh.

"Do not fear, boy. Your pain will be ending very soon. Very soon indeed," Plumb whispered, walking up to where he lay.

She kicked him into an empty grave.

Rain filled the bottom of the deep cavity, and Moony's body lay sinking into the muddy floor. Above, storm clouds swirled, churning dark secrets.

Plumb appeared at the mouth of the grave. She now looked nothing like the gentle baker Moony had known all his life. She was an entirely new creature. Moony suddenly understood the reason for the jars of flesh in the upstairs bedroom of the bakery. It was to mask her rot—the rot caused by Malivar's presence within her.

"Hobble is doomed," Plumb hissed triumphantly. "I have heard whispers of a savior to come, but I see no one here to save you now. The Vothlor are rising. Even the prisoner in the watchtower has escaped. As you saw, he has taken his stagecoach to retrieve the phantom armies. The wrath Malivar will unleash on your people has only just begun. He will send plague upon plague against Hobble! The War Of Souls has finally begun!"

Plumb hovered down from the lip of the grave, and floated above Moony, as if she were going to lay down upon him.

"The son of a murderer! The grandson of that worm Pottleman! What hope do you have for *true* greatness, boy? Receive the mark. Let Malivar live in you, and you will never have to die."

Moony imagined a life without fear of death. A life without end.

Plumb spread her fingers into the mark of a $\mathbf{V}$, and extended her hand towards Moony's neck. A simple act of submission, and he would never have to fear death again.

"I'd rather die than join the Vothlor," Moony finally replied. "My soul will rest in the Light."

Plumb hissed, "Then you're going to die! Just like your father died when he refused the mark. I found him wandering around in the watchtower with his silly maps, spying on the watchtower prisoner. Rest assured, your father suffered a most painful death. I paralyzed him with the same spell I used on the Gubbles, and his flesh and organs were eaten away by rats and fire ants. By now, he's nothing more than a skeleton in the watchtower. And now, it's your turn to join him."

She then unlocked her jaws and opened her mouth wide enough to place Moony's head deep inside her throat.

Chapter 30:

Act Of Desperation

As Plumb began closing her mouth around his head, Moony cringed in pain. Her bladed teeth sank into his neck, and creeks of blood trickled out of the tiny, slivered wounds. Fear rushed over him, blinding his senses, numbing his thoughts. He did not want to die—even if it was his destiny.

"Wait!" Moony pleaded from inside Plumb's mouth, feeling a rush of vengeance at Plumb's murder confession.

The baker ignored his plea, and continued closing her jaws.

"Wait! Wait! If you kill me, then you won't find the other children! I'm the only one who knows where they are!"

Plumb slowly withdrew Moony's head from her mouth.

"Tell me," she demanded.

Moony's heart chugged as he lay face to face with

Plumb.

Right then, he looked up and saw an owl sitting atop a nearby mausoleum—the same mausoleum in which Pappy Cricklewood had been interred a few days before. The owl's yellow eyes stared at Moony, and the boy felt an unexplainable surge of courage within his heart.

"Let me out of this grave, and I'll take you there," he promised Plumb. "You can give them all the mark. You just have to let me and my sister go free."

Plumb caressed her rotting face, and flakes of grey skin fluttered off her cheeks and sprinkled onto Moony's bloodstained shirt. Malivar's voice within her had commanded her to filter through Hobble's future mothers, fathers, craftsmen, shopkeepers, and Elders so the last tribe of the Lostwood would be extinguished once and for all.

Only those who would receive the mark of the ⚡ willingly would survive.

Plumb taunted Moony, "Quick to betray those who have done you no harm, aren't you? Let's play a game, shall we? If you lead me to the children, I'll let you and your sister live. But if they are not where you say they are, I will start with your toes and work my way up to your juicy little eyes."

She awaited Moony's response.

"It's—it's a deal. I'll show you where they are," he said softly, fighting guilt.

Plumb tasted Moony's bleeding face with her slimy, black tongue, and hovered back to the ledge of the muddy grave.

"Know this, boy: Hobble will not win this war. The

132

Black Candle has already been divided so that it can never be extinguished again. You may as well choose the side that will win, so you can enjoy the spoils of Malivar's power."

She raised Moony's body out of the grave and placed him standing on the ground.

Her flesh was now entirely grey and rotten. A few patches of stringy, white hair hung over her black-diamond eyes.

"Lead the way," the creature commanded, digging her black fingernail into Moony's back.

Without another word, Moony took off into the wild night sky with the vessel of Malivar on his heels.

Chapter 31:

Betrayal

Moony and Plumb descended into the Lostwood, landing at the mouth of the cave of skulls.

"Don't play games with me, boy. I smelled no children at this cave before," Plumb hissed.

"I hid them all before the Gubbles arrived," Moony explained, shivering in the downpour.

The dark creature looked over Moony's shoulder into the mouth of the rocky cave. The Gubble sisters still stood inside the dim chamber, imprisoned by Plumb's spell.

"Show me where they are, and I will let you and your sister go free," Plumb promised.

Moony considered the truce.

"The kids—they're—" Moony hesitated for just a moment. "Look right above you—in the trees."

Plumb smiled at the dozens of waxed children cradled in the thicket of limbs above.

"No wonder I could not smell them. Those traitorous witches used a spell to block their scent," she whispered. "An old witch's brew."

Plumb flew up into the limbs and approached the first child.

Moony was silent as the fiend dug her claws into the waxed body of Oakie Slugtroff, right where the boy's heart would be.

Plumb chewed through the boy's waxed head, and Moony cringed in horror at Oakie's unjust death.

"Why don't you fight me instead?!" Moony shouted. "If I win, then the children live. If you win, you can do with them as you wish."

Plumb considered it for a moment, then flew down to the ground.

Spiders crawled out of her mouth and ran down her body towards the dead grass beneath her feet. Moony could not tell if the spiders were real, or placed in his mind as a nightmare.

Plumb growled, "I will begin with your legs, and let the blood leak out of you while you watch the other children choose, one by one. I will even pick my teeth with your sister's bones if she denies the mark."

She crept toward Moony. For every step he took backwards toward the mouth of the cave, Plumb took two steps forward.

Suddenly, the terrible creature once known as Plumb raised her arms up to the storm, and shouted to the sky, "I offer my entire being to you! Fill me, Master Malivar! Let your powers flow through me!"

Lightning splintered down from the clouds, and

entered her fingertips. She lit up like a bonfire of demons, and Moony could see the black skeleton within her. Her flesh melted, and she transformed into the image of a cloaked vapor. Inside the vapor floated only Plumb's black skeleton.

Now, a new voice came from the creature's mouth. A darker voice.

"Join me. Receive the mark. I will make you more powerful than you can imagine. You will never have to die."

Moony now knew Plumb was gone, and only Malivar existed within her.

"I'll never join you," Moony replied. "I will die before I ever let you inside of me."

"Then die you will," Malivar promised, calmly.

Immediately, flames burst out of Malivar's fingertips and lit the trunk of the tree on fire. Moony could see that waxed faces of the children beginning to glisten in the heat.

Moony froze in fright as Malivar wrapped his vaporous fingers around his neck. A dark fire brewed in the darkness within the cloak. Moony tried to fly away, but felt paralyzed in his grasp.

Malivar squeezed Moony's neck. The stinging scent of Death poured out of Malivar's rotten gullet and burned Moony's eyes and nostrils. Spiders, worms, and dark shadows squirmed within the slimy, black abyss.

I want your soul, Moony Jarman, the voice spoke into Moony's thoughts. *You fear death, but with me you shall never die. I can give you all things. Receive the mark, and become everlasting.*

Malivar's vaporous arm reached for Moony's neck, waiting on the boy to make his final decision—death, or joining the Vothlor for eternity. He smelled the smoke and felt the heat of the burning tree, and knew he did not have much time.

"I'll destroy you!" Moony said, enraged. "You killed my father, and I won't let you harm anyone else."

That's it, boy. Let your rage guide you. Let it boil inside you until your heart is blackened, Malivar's voice whispered in Moony's thoughts

Suddenly, the Luminary began to glow inside Moony's chest, and a bright, blue current flooded through his veins. A peculiar force outside of Moony moved his trembling hand to the leather handle of his sword and lifted it from its scabbard.

It was by no mere strength of his own that Moony lifted the blade into the air.

"You?!" Malivar cried out, looking beyond Moony.

Moony looked over his shoulder, and was shocked by who he saw standing next to him.

"Be strong, boy. I'm with you," Mayor Waddletub encouraged, as he gripped the sword alongside Moony.

The void beneath Malivar's hood grew darker as he raised his vaporous fingertips. A purple storm fired out of his hands and deflected off the saber without harming Moony or the mayor. The sword shook in Moony's grip as he felt an unexplainable surge of power flow through him.

Moony and the mayor raised the sword against Malivar, but he stopped it in mid-air, struggling against the power of the Light.

"I cannot be destroyed as long as the Black Candle remains lit and others carry me within them," Malivar strained, his cloak flapping in the storm. "My vessel has no reason to fear weapons made by mere Hobblers."

Suddenly, the sword began to glow, and a bright white fire hummed around its blade.

"Lucky for me, this sword was forged by my grandfather—a Jypsi," Moony declared.

Then, as quick as an axe through a rotted log, the saber sliced through the cloak. The dark vapor dissolved, and the fire in the tree was immediately extinguished. Out of the vapor, a decrepit, black skull rolled across the puddle ground, and came to stop against the mound of skulls.

As soon as the head touched the pile of skulls, tiny explosions of light wrapped around the mound of bones. Streams of lightning whispered through the hollow eye sockets and empty mouths of the forgotten children who had been slaughtered long ago. Each of the skulls slowly dissolved into vapor, which floated into the flickering clouds above.

All that was left was the black skull of the baker once known as Plumb.

Right then, the Clock Tower struck in the distance.

Midnight. Exactly one month after Mayor Waddletub had lit the glitter cannons at the Star Festival.

Suddenly, the storm died down. The wind stopped howling.

Moony and the mayor exchanged a look of awe and relief.

"How did you know we'd be here?" Moony asked.

"I came to check on the Gubbles and the children, to make sure everything was in place. When I arrived in the cave and saw the waxed children were gone, and that the Gubbles were spellbound, I knew something was wrong. So I hid and waited. Then you and our old friend Plumb arrived, and I understood what had happened. *She* was the vessel. Because of recent—" Mayor Waddletub paused, and chose his words wisely, "Because of recent *happenings* these past months, I had long suspected that Malivar was hibernating within one of our own, but I never dreamed it was Plumb. It is hard to tell these things sometimes. Luckily for us, Malivar wasn't yet at full strength within her. Things could have been much worse. Alas, I fear this war has only just begun."

"So Malivar is not dead?" Moony questioned.

Mayor Waddletub smiled, as if Moony had much left to learn.

"No, Moony, he isn't. But you have succeeded upon this first trial."

Moony stared at the ground, then looked up at the mayor.

"But where have you been hiding all month?" Moony asked. "The whole town has been looking for you. We've needed you."

"I've been preparing for what is to come. Tell no one you've seen me, Moony, and I will not tell them *your* secret. Let them believe whatever they need to believe about me for the time being. In the end, all will be set right. The Jypsis are even saying there is a

Promised One who will help Hobble in the dark times to come."

Moony remained silent.

"I must go now. I trust you'll help guide the children back to Hobble?" Mayor Waddletub asked.

Moony nodded, and the brave mayor trundled off into the Lostwood.

Moony looked up at the waxed children in the tree above him. The wax shells were beginning to melt, and Moony knew that Jezzy was safe. He also knew he had to get out of sight before he was seen by the Gubbles or by any of the awakened children.

But first . . .

Moony flew to the mouth of the cave, and picked up Plumb's skull. It was as cold as Death, and a hundred cockroaches fled from its innards. He held the skull up into the torchlight, his thumb in the black hollow of her mouth and his fingers wrapped in her brittle eye sockets.

Then, after tucking the evil relic under his arm, he quickly flew up into the calming night, and set out to hide the skull in a place where it would never be found—at the Protector's Sanctuary.

And for a brief moment, the moon peeked through the midnight clouds, and twelve ghosts materialized at the edge of the woods just outside the cave, drifting back to the Tree Of the Dead.

Epilogue:

A Merry Return To Hobble

A few moments after the Clock Tower's twelfth strike, the Gubble sisters were released from Plumb's spell. The three looked at one another in confusion, unable to remember anything of the previous hour. They peered around the empty cave, and realized that Plumb had somehow been defeated.

Nearby, behind the boulder, the potato sack squirmed anxiously. Issa ran over and carefully unlaced the twine ties as two hands peeled open the bag from within. A wiry-haired, goggle-eyed boy emerged, and yelped in horror at the sight of the Gubble sisters.

"Calm down, boy. There is nothing to be afraid of. The terror has passed," Issa soothed in a gentle voice.

"Get away from me! I don't trust a word you say!" Starflyer Stevens replied, stepping away from his captors.

He looked around at the cave.

"Where are we?" he asked, awed by the chamber.

"This is an ancient goblin cave, not far from the Light Mines," Gertrude answered. "Don't worry. We'll have you home in no time."

There was a rustling outside the cave, and dozens of children climbed down from the now-blackened tree where Moony had hid them. The freed captives trembled at the strange, frightful sights of the Lostwood, and wiped the soot from their faces.

The Gubbles heard the children outside the cave, and rushed to meet them.

"Don't be afraid, children. The Darkness has passed tonight. Your lives have been spared."

Huff Howler stepped forward from the crowd of dazed children, and shouted, "You're the ones who nabbed us while we were playing Goblinlight!"

He quickly turned and motioned for the other children to stay away from the Gubbles.

"Yeah, you're the ones who stuffed me into your cellar!" the boy who was as skinny as a noodle proclaimed.

The mob of kids slowly backed away from the sisters in suspicion.

"It was for your own safety!" Issa explained. "While you were asleep, Malivar came to offer you the mark of the ⫯, but he can no longer harm you. We knew Malivar was coming for you tonight, though we did not know in what vessel he would appear. So we prepared an ancient recipe. The brew you sipped in the bakery was an enchanted potion to keep away the nightmares and preserve you within a wax shell, where your scent could not be traced by Malivar. Alas, I'm afraid it was Plumb, the beloved town baker, who was carrying Malivar within her. Your mothers and fathers never would have understood, nor would they have been able to protect you. This was the only way. You must trust what we say. Your nightmares are over—for now at least."

Huff and the others examined the Gubble sisters with suspicious glares.

But one girl in a pink dress stepped out from the crowd.

"I believe you," Jezzy Jarman announced.

After a few silent moments, more of the children sensed the sisters were telling the truth.

Just then, Sheriff, Deputy, and Fink Karbunkle, a retired pumpkin farm, ran out of the dark forest.

"I found them!" Sheriff shouted, nudging Deputy with his elbow. "I told you I'd be the one to find the missing kids!"

Deputy rolled his eyes, and turned to Issa Gubble.

"I saw Stokely Scabbins leave through the gates without a pass an hour ago, and we followed the tracks of that boogeywagon she was ridin' in. I guess you could say we're—we're heroes."

Issa smiled, and softly touched Deputy's badge. She then leaned in, kissed his cheek, and his face turned bright red.

"Golly, Miss Gubble. There's—there are children watching," Deputy said, bashfully.

"Children, are you alright?" Fink Karbunkle asked, a wealth of dark memories overwhelming him at the sight of the cave.

"I think we're safe now that you're here," Jezzy replied, taking Fink's hand. "Can we go back home now?"

Fink smiled down at the little one, and said, "Yes, dear heart. I will take you home."

Just then, branches crunched in the nearby woods, and a shadow-faced man ran out of the dark forest. He wore a black bandana over his mouth and nose, and a short-brimmed conductor's hat atop his head. His eyes were smoky red, like two foggy suns. Starflyer had seen the conductor of the Light Train at the Light Dock only a few days before. The man looked at the children and the Gubbles with puzzled surprise.

"What in da kittens' whiskers are y'all doin' out here? Never seen such a sight. We saw lightnin' striking the forest in these here parts, and I came to make sure there wasn't no wildfire spreadin'."

Gertrude stepped forward and addressed the man in a flirtatious whisper, "Dear sir, is your train on its way to Hobble perchance?"

She batted her eyelashes at him playfully, but the conductor coldly examined her from head to toe, and replied in an unfriendly whisper, "I know your kind, witch, and I ain't fallin' for your snares." He looked at the children. "But I reckon you little ones need a ride back to town, eh?"

The conductor brushed past Gertrude, swept two children up into his arms, and carried them toward the Light Train puffing in the near distance. The remaining children ran after the conductor, excited at the prospect of a train ride through the mysterious Lostwood.

Moments later, all the children were welcomed into the lantern-lit cars of the Light Train. Miners distributed wool blankets and mugs of hot cocoa to warm the children on their ride back to town. As the train's wheels began to roll along the tracks, the children sipped from their mugs and sang folksongs.

Except for one boy.

When Starflyer Stevens was following the other children to the Light Train, he had caught sight of something hidden in the bumpkin bushes. An amazed smile grew across his lips as he walked over to his Starwagon.

That's strange, he thought. *Why would the Starwagon be parked way out here near a cave? Maybe Botty left it here for me?*

The young inventor wiped the driver's seat with the tail of his labcoat and jumped in. In the near distance, the Light Train whistled, and Starflyer followed after it like a bumblebee, zipping around trees and soaring over ditches all the way back to Hobble.

Where hundreds of Hobblers lay in bed dreaming strange, haunted dreams.

The Light Train puffed as it ascended onto the southern wall of town.

Colorful streams of light flickered up and down the side panels of the steel beast like a vibrant rainbow. The locomotive squealed to a stop directly above the Light Dock, and the conductor slithered out the front window of the train and somersaulted down to the dock below. A dozen shadow-faced miners emerged from the train cars, and hitched slides from the train cars down to the Light Dock. One by one, the children slid down the slides, and sucked the chilly Hobble air into their lungs.

All of them felt as if they had finally arrived at the end of a long, strange dream.

The swarm of children quickly burst apart from one another like a festival firework, and scattered to their cottages and farmhouses, knocking on the doors of darkened porches and waking their mothers and fathers with joyful cheers. All across Hobble, candelabras were lit, curtains were pulled back, and excited faces appeared in the windows of twinkling cottages. The worries of a hundred troubled parents melted away at the return of their happy, sooty-faced children. Fathers and mothers hugged their beloved children and smothered them with kisses.

All the while, the Fiddler played the merriest song he had played all month long . . .

Hoot Cricklewood let out a wild yelp, and sprinted toward the Museum Of Wonders.

He could not wait to tell Notch, Garth, and Pappy what had happened to him and how brave he'd been. Hoot pulled open the giant doors of the museum, ran down the hallway, and up the creaking stairwell to wake his father.

At the sound of Hoot's voice, Garth sat up in bed and clutched his pillow to his chest. When he saw his youngest son standing in the doorway, he half-believed the boy to be an apparition. The dazed father tumbled out of bed and held his arms out to Hoot, who fell into his embrace.

Hoot explained everything to his father, who listened with dismay—and guilt—to the boy's rapid rambling. Then Hoot asked, "Dad, let's wake Notch and Pappy! I've gotta tell 'em everything that's happened!"

Garth placed a gentle hand on Hoot's shoulder, and took a deep breath.

The museum director spoke softly, "Hoot, I don't know where Notch is. Haven't seen him all night. I hoped he had returned with the rest of you. But, Hoot—" Garth paused before he attempted to explain the unthinkable tragedy which had occurred only a few days before. "Hoot, Pappy is gone. And he won't be coming back. We buried him in the graveyard two days ago."

Hoot's eyes dimmed with sadness, "What—what do you mean?"

Garth placed his other hand on Hoot's shoulder and carefully explained, "Pappy—well, you see, Pappy went where all things go when they die. But he's still with us, Hoot. He'll always be with us—just like the Hobble Star."

Garth pointed up through the skylight of his bedroom to the center of the night sky. The Hobble Star flickered above, showering them with its perpetual light.

Starflyer zoomed through the Crescent Gates and drove straight to his family's house on the western side of town. He was pleasantly surprised when both of his parents opened the thrice-locked door and embraced him with eager hugs.

"Son, oh Son, where have you been?" Orson Jr. questioned.

Starflyer took a deep breath, and attempted to explain, "It was Plumb, Dad! All along, Plumb was part of the Vothlor! She tried to give us all the mark, but the Gubbles saved all the kids by hiding us in a cave in the Lostwood.

We'd all be dead if it weren't for them."

Orson Jr. sighed. "So it's true then. There are still Vothlor *vessels*. I'll find each one of them, and as sure as I'm standing here, they'll be sent to the gallows where they belong."

Starflyer nodded.

Not much has changed since I've been away, he thought.

He looked back over his shoulder at the Critchfield Mansion looming on the distant hill. Smoke rose out of its chimney, and a solitary light burned in the Moontower. Starflyer slowly lifted a hand and waved, believing the hermit might be watching, not knowing the hermit was far away from Hobble in that very moment.

"So are you going to go upstairs and say hello to your friend, Botty, or not?" Orson Jr. asked with a shy smile.

Starflyer grinned at his father, and bolted up the stairs to the attic laboratory.

On the other side of Hobble, at the edge of the pumpkin farm, Gabbo Scabbins counted ten of his children as they bounded into the Pumpkin House. But Gabbo's bright smile suddenly faded as he realized that his two oldest children, Scooter and Stokely, were not with the others.

Stokely Scabbins awoke to the echo of the Clock Tower's twelfth gong ringing in the distance.

"You there, Scooter?" Stokely whispered into the cold darkness.

She heard a rustling nearby.

"I'm over here," Scooter replied. His shoulders stung in pain, and he felt dozens of tiny wounds in his skin, as if he had been bitten. But he was alive, and for that, he was grateful.

Stokely crawled across the cold ground toward her brother's voice.

"Where are we?" Scooter asked, still in a daze.

"Don't know," Stokely confessed. "Maybe we're still in the cave?"

"What cave?" Scooter questioned. The last thing he remembered was being captured by the Gubbles in the tunnels.

"Nevermind," Stokely replied, knowing Scooter would never believe her about Plumb or that Moony Jarman could fly. "I'll tell you all about it later."

Scooter continued rummaging around in the darkness.

"What are you doing, Scoot?" Stokely asked.

"I found our torch," Scooter replied.

Using their flints, the torch erupted into a simmering glow which revealed both Scooter's face . . .

And the skull of a skeleton.

Stokely jumped back at the sight of the skull's cobwebbed eye sockets. A cross-belt with a diamond at the center was strapped over the torso bones. She then noticed a name burned into the skeleton's satchel—*Joseph Jarman.*

"It can't be," she whispered in puzzlement. "Is this—are we back in the watchtower? And this—could this be Moony and Jezzy's father who disappeared a while back after—?"

"Look!" Scooter pointed at the ground.

There was the symbol outlined in the heel of each footprint—a haunting **V**. The footprints trailed around a hole in the floor and stopped right next to an arched doorway.

"The Golden Door," Stokely whispered in wonder.

The twins brushed away the thick tangle of spider webs and tapped a few times on the cold door. It sounded hollow on the other side.

"It looks like someone already tried to open the door—maybe it was the prisoner who Pappy Cricklewood let escape. There must be something in here that Silas wants. Think of it: he spent all those years in that cell, only a few feet away from this door. Must have been pretty disappointed when he found out he couldn't get in there," Scooter said, pointing to the blade marks next to the keyhole.

"The key to the Omni!" Stokely said excitedly, remembering the secret conversation she had overheard in the tunnels below only a few hours before.

"Quick, Scooter. Where's the key?"

Scooter searched his trouser pockets, pulled out the key, and handed it to Stokely.

The twins exchanged an excited glance, and then Stokely inserted the key into the lock and turned it. To their surprise, the door creaked open. A cold, dusty draft breathed out of the room and chilled their faces.

Together, the twins stepped through the arched doorway, held the torch light up into the darkness, and discovered something more incredible and unexpected than anything they had ever seen.

Moony staggered out of the Lostwood and through the unguarded Crescent Gates. He covered his wounds the best he could, so no Hobblers would grow suspicious of his beaten and bloody appearance.

He made his way through the shadowed lanes, heading back to the refuge of his barn loft. Along the way, he stopped in the alley behind the bakery and looked up into its orange-tinted window. There, he saw the three silhouettes of the Gubble sisters packing their things to return to the mountain from which they had come. But the Vothlor had returned, and for himself he knew that his duties as Protector had only just begun.

Moony smiled to himself, and trudged toward the inn where Jezzy, Gem, and Beatrice awaited him.

After everyone in Hobble had gone back to sleep, the witching hour filled the town with a haunting silence. Trees stood still, stars remained hidden behind motionless clouds, and not a critter or creature stirred in the night.

Garth Cricklewood relieved Deputy Notwod of his gatekeeping duties, as he had done each night for the previous month. But the Deputy had forgotten one important task of the night. The museum caretaker whistled a lonely tune, while thinking of his son, Notch, who had not returned to Hobble with the other children. Garth pondered over the mystery of his son's absence as he climbed up the left wall of the Crescent Gates and, upholding the monthly tradition of the gatekeepers, blew out the first of twelve lanterns.

The first October of the year was already over, and a new one had begun.

A spiral of smoke ascended from the wick and dispelled into the night. The other eleven lanterns remained shimmering in the cold darkness, just as Happy and Guffy had left them.

Garth sat down in the creaky gatekeeper's chair, and flipped open his father's pocketknife. He produced a stick from his shirtfront pocket and began to whittle it into a toothpick to pass the time, while reminiscing over his many memories of Pappy. Suddenly, he stopped, sensing something strange lingering in the night.

He heard the thudding sound of footsteps approaching, and looked back toward the sleeping town.

Someone was approaching the Crescent Gates from the direction of Town Hall. Garth stood up, surprised by the late-night visitor.

"Garth Cricklewood, I have a letter for you," a woman's voice spoke from the shadows of the creeping fog.

Garth squinted his eyes, trying to recognize the face of his visitor. A familiar visage appeared in the soft light cast down by the eleven remaining crescent lanterns.

Mayor Humplestock stepped out of the fog and stood before Garth. Her face was expressionless, and her silver hair gleamed in the moonlight.

She handed him a crinkled, yellowed envelope, which he hesitantly took into his hands.

"This letter was entrusted to Town Hall fifty years ago, with the instructions that it be delivered to you at this exact moment, in this exact place, after the blowing out of the first crescent lantern," Mayor Humplestock continued.

Garth trembled at the revelation.

When he glanced back up, Mayor Humplestock was already strolling back toward Town Hall.

Garth cautiously peeled open the seal of the envelope with Pappy's pocketknife, and wondered how the letter could have possibly been written to him before he was born. Then he removed the leaf of paper from within, and read Notch's familiar handwriting aloud:

Beware your destinies.
The Dark Circus is coming.

FIND OUT WHAT HAPPENS NEXT IN ...

VOLUME TWO:
THE DARK CIRCUS

-COMING SOON-

DARE TO UNLOCK THE MYSTERIES.
READ ALL FOUR BOOKS TO SOLVE THE VANISHING

BOOK 1:
THE
TIME CRYSTAL

BOOK 2:
THE
HERMIT'S MANSION

BOOK 3:
THE
WATCHTOWER SECRET

BOOK 4:
THE
PROTECTOR'S EMERALD

Become a citizen of Hobble!

Visit

www.theoctobers.com

to receive your citizenship papers and
enter the OCTOBERS contests!

MOONSUNG
presents

FOR UPCOMING TITLES, VISIT:

WWW.MOONSUNGBOOKS.COM

Author websites:

J.H. Reynolds: www.moonsungbooks.com

Craig Cunningham: www.craigcunningham.blog.com